Praise for *Cry Wolf*

"What seems, at first, a gentle fable about farm animals who enjoy a kind of ordered liberty, turns quickly into a grim allegory about man's dark impulse toward the collective."

—Laurie Morrow
Political Columnist, *The Montpelier Bridge*

"A charming and chilling fable that underscores the fragility of a world achieved with great difficulty and so easily undone by good intentions gone awry."

—Richard John Neuhaus
Editor in Chief, *First Things*

"*Cry Wolf* is one of those masterpieces of fable that seem inevitable once they have appeared, but that take genius and luck to discover in the first place. . . . *Cry Wolf* is a must-read for anyone thinking seriously about the nature of community and the cultural and spiritual underpinnings of productive political order. The book is a profound thought experiment about the limits of inclusiveness, the fragility of civility, and the meaning of 'we' and 'they.'

It is also an astonishing work of art, written by one of the nation's greatest living poets, worthy to stand with the darkest parables of Aristophanes, Aesop, Swift, Kafka, and Orwell. The characters are unforgettably endearing or terrifying; the topicality is blatant; the atmosphere compelling; the plotting an exquisitely crafted combination of suspense, foreboding irony, hilarious black comedy, and satirical wit.

This book will surely become an essential reference and proverbial feature in any future discussion of what it means to have a border."

—Frederick Turner
Founders Professor of Arts and Humanities,
the University of Texas at Dallas

CRY WOLF

—

A Political Fable

Paul Lake

BENBELLA BOOKS, INC.
Dallas, TX

BenBella Books, Inc.
10440 N. Central Expressway, Suite 800
Dallas, TX 75231
Send feedback to feedback@benbellabooks.com
www.benbellabooks.com

BenBella is a federally registered trademark.

Printed in the United States of America

Library of Congress Cataloging-in-Publication Data
Lake, Paul, 1951–
  Cry wolf : a political fable / Paul Lake.
      p. cm.
  ISBN 1-933771-42-9
  1. Political fiction. I. Title.

  PS3562.A379C79 2008
  813'.54—dc22

                        2008009670

Proofreading by Maggie McGuire, Robbie Garvin, and Stacia Seaman
Cover design by Laura Watkins
Cover painting by J. P. Targete
Design and composition by PerfecType, Nashville, TN

Special discounts for bulk sales are available. Please contact
bulkorders@benbellabooks.com.

For Tina, as always

ACKNOWLEDGMENTS

I would like to thank all of the people who helped in the creation of this book: first, my wife, Tina, for her encouragement and support; my son, Alex, who urged me to write it, gave me ideas, and read it first; my inspired agent, Cathy Hemming of Sanford J. Greenburger Associates; proofreader extraordinaire Donna White for her help and encouragement; Earl Schrock for his farming tips; and all of my friends, colleagues, and students at Arkansas Tech, who encouraged and supported me, especially Carl Brucker, my department chairman, who has done so much to support my endeavors over the years.

CHAPTER 1

Shep walked through the empty farmhouse, claws clicking on the hardwood floors, till he reached the back of the house, where a scent of peppermint and tobacco wafted from a flannel coat hanging on a wooden peg by the door.

Shep squeezed through the swinging flap at the door's base and emerged on the other side into crisp autumn air.

A breeze ruffled the fur at his neck as he looked across the barnyard where chickens and geese were already bustling about, preparing for the night's entertainment.

Suddenly, a tall gray goose ran flapping across the yard, honking excitedly in his direction.

"Better come, better come. There's been a breach in Sheep's Meadow. Hurry, hurry, hurry," she called.

With a flutter of wings, Gertrude pulled up in front of Shep and gasped, "Better get out there. There's blood, blood on the ground. The sheep are starting to panic."

Shep eyed the goose calmly. Gert was a fierce protector of the barnyard, but like most geese, prone to excitement. He gave her a moment to gather her wits, then turned toward the distant meadow and sniffed the air.

The wind was blowing from the east, bearing a trace of damp wool and sheep droppings. No trace of blood, though. Still, Shep thought, he'd better have a look, or Gert would worry him silly.

"I'll check the pasture," he said. "Keep the gates clear. I've got to bring the sheep in for the pageant."

Gert arched her neck and gave him a searching look. "Well, I must say, you're taking this calmly. Nothing to worry about. Sorry to bother. Perhaps it's only a bear."

She turned abruptly and waddled away, still honking and shaking her head.

Shep nosed the breeze again, then bounded off toward the pasture. Skirting the garden, he rounded the orchard, where a few shriveled apples lay rotting on the ground beneath rows of bare-limbed trees.

As he passed the orchard, two pigs suddenly emerged, still chewing half-rotten apples.

"Where ya off to?" asked Barlow with a friendly smack of his lips. His chin glistened with sticky juice. "The wife and I were just having a little repast before the evening's festivities."

Shep wrinkled his nose but maintained a polite demeanor. Pigs were filthy animals, if left to wallow in their sty. The trick was to keep them busy, working the farm and tending to their chores. As a result of such efforts, Barlow and Bertha were rather lean and tidy, as pigs go. Still, they bore looking after.

"We've had a breach," Shep said. "I thought I'd have a look. And anyway, the sheep will need a nip or two to get them in on time."

"Poor dim dears," Bertha sniffed. "Haven't got the sense to come in out of a hailstorm. Bless their hearts."

As the pigs ambled away toward the barnyard, Shep headed toward the cattle pasture, where a few scattered Herefords were grazing on the last remnants of autumn grass. Garth, the large bull who ruled the herd, stood humped in the center of the field, silent and still as stone. Despite his impressive size and curving horns, he was a dull fellow with an exaggerated sense of his own importance. To avoid him, Shep edged along the barbed wire fence, scouting for trouble and marking fence posts as he passed.

At a place where a giant oak overreached the fence, he paused to look at a sign nailed to the trunk.

NO TRESPASSING.

Once, when two hunters and their dogs had strayed onto the farm, Shep had accompanied Grover to this spot to confront the intruders. Pointing to the sign with his gun barrel, the old man let them know just what it meant. Today, when the valley's farms were failing all around them, hunters no longer strayed onto their property or fired guns in the surrounding woods.

Still, every animal on the farm knew what that sign meant and would risk its hide or feathers to enforce its message.

Shep followed the fence line till it dipped into a gully where it crossed a stream that snaked through the meadow into the tree-covered hills beyond.

The stream was a great asset to the farm, assuring it a steady supply of water, but was a constant threat to security. Erosion undermined the fence posts, and floods battered its wires with floating debris. When the stream was low, a gap formed between the fence and waterline big enough for a bear to crawl through.

Today its muddy banks were etched with fresh hoofprints. As Shep approached, he smelled the rich scent of deer. He leaned closer to get a better sniff, and his nostrils caught the coppery scent of blood.

Gert was right, they'd had a visitor. A doe—young but seasoned, and but for her wound, in reasonably good health. Shep could gather that much from spoor and blood. He tracked the scent up the bank into the meadow, then circled back where it vanished in the stream.

Wounded or healthy, the doe posed little threat. Though a small herd could soon deplete a field, a lone deer was just a nuisance. If she returned, the cows could drive her away. Shep galloped beside the fence across the pasture till it turned north, then abandoned it to round up the scattered sheep.

Bounding across the grass, he yipped sharply to alert them of his intent. Then he swept in fast and low and nipped at a few heels to startle the flock into motion.

"Come on, ladies, no dawdling, step lively there."

To a border collie, a flock of sheep was like a mound of wet clay, to be molded into whatever shape he chose. Shep darted across the grass, flashing his teeth and feinting toward stragglers, till he had the whole flock moving with a single mind.

"Step lively, or I'll leave you out here with the coyotes. That's right, follow the leader. Single file."

"Ca-ca-coyotes or not," bleated an indignant ewe, "you don't have to *nip*. We're moving along rather nicely now."

No coyote had ever been seen in these parts, but the thought put some life into reluctant hooves and haunches. Within minutes Shep had the whole flock galloping across the fields on a track to the barn.

When they reached the barnyard, the sheep scattered among the crowd of spectators jockeying for position near the stage.

This was the first harvest festival they'd ever held. In their last summer meeting, the Animal Council had decided to hold it this time each fall to celebrate the harvest and commemorate their heroic victory. Now that the day was here, the animals were milling about, unsure what to expect.

A large gray stallion named Kit stood near the back of the crowd, flicking his tail, while Mara, May, and Moll, his three mares, shuffled about, complaining of the delay. Eudora and the other cows stood beside the pigs, Barlow and Bertha, who lay on their bellies, chatting with passing hens.

At last, the crowd settled and the actors took their places. The young colts, chicks, and goslings stood in a semicircle facing the audience, waiting for the director's cue. At a nod from Gert, they stood up straight and put on solemn faces. Then to delighted *oohs* and *ahs*, a tall black calf stepped forward and boldly addressed the crowd.

"This is how the animals of Green Pastures Farm became free and self-governing citizens. This is how we learned to farm the land and protect our sacred borders."

CHAPTER 2

"First," bawled the calf over the heads of the crowd, "Evelyn, the gray-haired mother, passed away and was taken to the land of the dead. As the days passed, our caretaker Grover grew weak and infirm, drawn by sadness to the earth's breast like a child. Instead of two legs, he walked on three. Then he stopped walking altogether and stayed in the man-house, not rising to tend the animals in his care.

"When he passed from the land of the living to the dead, no men or motors came to take him away, so Mara bore him from the house on her strong back, and we made a hole in the earth and laid him in it.

"Then one moonless night, the lights on the farm went out. The windows became dark pools, the house was silent. It was as if night had come to stay forever. Fear descended on our hearts like dew on summer grass.

"A tumult of wild voices rose from barn and stable. The air echoed with lamentations. In our sorrow and despair, confusion reigned. "

His part completed, the calf stepped back to rejoin the chorus behind him, and a half-grown lamb stepped forward to resume the tale.

"But in the midst of confusion," he baa-ed softly, "a wise cow named Eudora admonished the others, saying, 'This time of fear and confusion must come to an end. We are not beasts of the forest who live alone and rely on chance for survival, but wise domestic animals who know the comfort of a stall and the wisdom of herding together. We have lived among men and women and grown tame at their hands. We are wise in the ways of living. We know that to eat in the winter, we must sow seeds in the spring and gather their fruit in summer. Let us put our heads together and think how to maintain ourselves and preserve the life of the farm.'"

"So an assembly was formed in the barnyard," said a gosling, stepping forward with a timid bow. "A council was chosen from among the wisest and, after consultations, said to all, 'Let us do the work ourselves that was once done by men. Though we have no strong machines and lack men's hands and cunning, we are strong and tireless in our labors. Working together, a hundred beaks and hooves and paws can match the might of a man and his machines.'

"And so when winter passed and the animals had eaten the corn and hay stored by man's hand, they plowed the ground with hooves and beaks and claws. They planted the seeds that had been stored by human hands and waited through days and nights for them to ripen. With unceasing vigilance, they guarded their fields from crows, groundhogs, and rabbits. When their time came and crops hung heavy on stalk and vine, they gathered their harvest from the fields with their great strength, dragging sacks and sledges and filling sheds and silos, to store against winter's famine."

"And in their f-foresight and wisdom," stuttered a nervous little piglet, "they saved some seeds and grain for the next year's planting. They dried apples in the sun and gathered sacks of sunflower seeds, then hid them in metal b-bins where the mice couldn't find them."

With a sigh of relief, the piglet stepped back into the chorus.

Then Gert took center stage, stretched out her wings, and proclaimed her words like a trumpet.

"But a terrible danger waited beyond our borders. No man-smell remained to deter the wild beasts there. The terrible thunder of man's guns was now silent. Beyond the borders of the farm, bandit-eyed raccoons and scheming groundhogs waited for us to falter in our tasks. Ravenous weasels and sharp-toothed foxes prowled our borders, dreaming of a festival of blood. Only our watchful eyes and loud alarms prevented their daily incursions. Only the thunder of our stamping hooves and wings drove them back into the dark where hunger dwells.

"But a day came," she said more darkly, dropping her voice to a hush, "when our vigilance was not enough to save us. A new terror descended on our fields and pastures. From out of the dark forest, a young bear came. Dashing fence rails aside like twigs, he entered the pasture, thirsting for blood and hungry for living flesh."

In the front row, a mother hen squawked and nearly fainted as a half-grown pig shambled forward on the stage. Coated from head to toe in a layer of mud, he reared back on his hind legs and staggered forward, mimicking the awkward gait of a bear.

"But the farm animals were equal to the occasion," Gert continued in a voice now quavering with emotion. "Garth, the brave guardian of the meadows, sounded the alarm. He circled the cattle behind him and stood at their front with his great curved horns aimed at the foe. A battalion of sheep galloped from the neighboring field to reinforce the cattle. . . ."

As she spoke, a flock of chicks fluttered across the stage to represent the fiercely charging sheep.

"Then the geese and pigs, the rooster and hens came running from the barn with deafening battle cries. From the stables, Kit, the stallion, charged the foe with his stampeding herd of mares.

"By itself," Gert continued more softly, "no animal has the strength or courage to face such a foe.

"But together," she proclaimed, stretching her enormous wings for effect, "the animals formed a living battlement. The cattle snorted and stamped and tossed their spear-tipped heads. The sheep and feathered flocks formed a spearhead to arrest the bear's advance.

"Yet despite this impressive display of courage, the bear flashed his dagger teeth and sneered at the herd, doubting their might and resolve. His mighty shoulders rose up, and he pawed the air, lusting for blood and battle.

"Then suddenly Kit leapt forward to meet his charge. The stallion reared up and beat his hooves in the air like summer lightning. Garth pawed the earth and advanced with lowered horns. The dogs snapped at the bear's furry flanks, to confound and confuse him."

Gert paused to take a breath and eye the audience. "For an instant," she said, "the bear seemed to shrink from the hooves raining down from above. He dropped to all fours and looked toward the fence with a wistful, uncertain gaze, then turned and galloped away to the friendly forest.

"As the bushes closed behind his dusty haunches, our cheers rang across the fields and echoed off the hills and mountains. From that day forward, no bloodthirsty beast has ever dared to trespass past the borders of Green Pastures Farm."

Flushed with triumph, Gert retracted her wings and slumped into a bow. She held her pose for several seconds as the audience sat in unresponsive silence.

At last, a hoarse voice shouted from the rear, "No Trespassing!"

"No Trespassing," echoed another. And soon the cry was taken up by the crowd.

The discord resolved itself into a shouted chant that lasted several minutes, dissolving into scattered howls and whinnies that echoed off the dark walls of the night.

CHAPTER 3

As the shouting died down and the audience began drifting toward their evening stalls, a disgruntled voice muttered over the noise of shuffling hooves, "Will someone please tell me why the noblest and most sophisticated farm animal was not depicted at the scene of our greatest triumph?"

A large yellow duck, shoulders hunched in a gesture of bafflement, was pacing back and forth in the center of the yard.

"Was I not there, along with my brave mistresses, in the midst of the danger?

"Perhaps I was not at the front," he added sardonically, "among the large mammals, where the opportunities for heroism are more abundant. We are not all fortunate enough to be born with giant hooves and flashing teeth. Yet despite the considerable risk to my person, did I not, from my post at the left rear flank, insist that the enemy leave the farm at once? Did I not recommend that violence be deferred until we had discussed more sensible courses of action? Are my brave efforts at diplomacy now to be forgotten merely because none were wise enough to heed my counsels?"

The duck glared at the indifferent hindquarters of his departing neighbors.

"Instead of resorting to violence," he added more loudly, "we might have signed a treaty with the beast. We might have secured our safety and prosperity not merely for one night, but for future generations. Am I alone in regretting that missed opportunity? Am I alone in deploring such displays of arrogance and jingoistic pride?"

"Oh, shut up, Pierre," growled Barlow walking past. "If it hadn't been for Kit, you'd have been duck soup.

"Go home," he snorted. "There's a full moon tonight. Go home before the owls come out."

"But, but, but—" the duck stuttered with a quick glance overhead.

Then seeing the others drifting away, he gave a final shrug and waddled off toward the distant pond, still muttering over his shoulder.

In the center of the yard, Gert was shooing the young actors away toward their parents and home.

"Great job, Gert," said a rooster, strutting past. "I almost felt like I was back in that field again. Maybe someday our young ones will appreciate your lesson. That was quite a show. Very stirring."

"Indeed," Gert replied with a modest bow. "I had hoped our little play would be instructive. In fact, I'm already thinking about next season. I think I'll compose a little story about the forming of the first Animal Council. Yes, and the founding of our laws. Indeed, indeed, I believe I will," she said, absentmindedly scooting the last gosling toward the barn with a sweep of her broad wing.

"I'll set my mind right to it."

In the distance, Pierre was still quacking to the air, but as the dusk thickened, no one had the patience to listen to his disgruntled musings. Silently, the hens filed toward the henhouse on weary legs. Once inside, they mounted their roosts in order like well-trained troops, then settled down to a night of dreamless sleep, secure in the safety and comfort of the henhouse.

While the hens snored softly into their breasts, Raymond mounted his perch and surveyed his domain with a swell of pride and satisfaction. He didn't need Gert's pageant to remind him of his service to the farm. Courage was in his blood. Even in the old days, under human care, he'd faced his share of danger. A chicken coop was a magnet for thieves and killers of every stripe. There was hardly an animal alive that wouldn't steal an egg. In his short life, Raymond had killed a dozen rats, chased off platoons of crows, and stood in the shadows of circling hawks, defying death while the hens and chicks scattered to safety.

Once, on a hot August afternoon last summer, he'd fought an epic battle with a small but determined blacksnake, dodging its fangs and twisting coils and parrying with his razor beak. Finally, when both were panting from exhaustion, the snake missed with a badly aimed strike and Raymond leapt forward and jabbed out the reptile's eye. Then with his spur, he pinned its vile neck to the ground, where the snake squirmed for several minutes like a severed worm before dropping its head in the dust.

Even on Green Pastures Farm, the life of a rooster was no picnic. In addition to predators, domestic disputes demanded his constant attention. Hens were proud, vain creatures, fiercely jealous of their place in the pecking order. Sometimes the pecking would get out of hand and a hen would be bloodied. Then a kind of madness would possess the flock, and they'd hammer the poor thing to death in a murderous frenzy. More than once, Raymond had to jump into the middle of a fray to stop the mayhem before it got out of hand.

A rooster's life was an unending round of duties and obligations. Mornings, he'd mount the nearest fence post and make the hills ring with his cries. At dusk, he'd track the moon and stars across the sky, measuring their sweep through the heavens. When the signs were right, he advised the others when it was time to plant in spring or gather the autumn harvest.

Just this morning, for instance, while observing the southern horizon, Raymond noticed it was only a matter of days before the sun reached winter solstice and reversed its downward course. Soon the animals would be huddling together in the barn through the long dark nights of winter. Soon it would be time to prepare for their holiest day.

Tonight, though, Raymond was tired. It had been a long day, filled with alarms and capped by the excitement of the pageant. Dropping his head to his chest, he entered a dark silent void, where time seemed to stop and for an instant he all but ceased to exist. Then a shimmer of invisible rays tickled some delicate membrane inside his head. He startled awake and with a ruffle of feathers hopped from his roost to the ground and across the yard to the nearest fence post.

Seizing a lungful of cold morning air, he reared back and let loose a mighty cry that shook the autumn air like a Tibetan gong.

Soon afterward, a large pig walked by, carrying a bucket by the handle in his mouth.

"Mrnmph, Rmmnnd," he said, looking up.

Barlow stopped in the rooster's shadow and set the bucket on the ground. Then he stretched his jaw and repeated more clearly, "I said, 'Morning, Raymond.'"

Tipping the bucket, he dragged it across the ground, spilling a mound of seeds on the dirt.

This time of year, when insects were scarce, it was Barlow's job to scatter feed around the chicken coop each morning. Then while the hens ate, he gathered eggs from their deserted nests and placed them gently in the bucket.

"It's going to be clear today," Raymond announced, peering up at the pink morning sky. "Clear and cold, with a three-quarter moon tonight."

Raymond glanced toward the neighboring forest and said with a hint of sadness, "Pity the wild ones, with no roof or winter store for the coming days."

Barlow snorted. "Live by claw without the law and body and soul will starve."

He gave an appreciative snort at the proverb's wisdom, then picked up his egg-filled bucket, crossed the barnyard, and entered the barn's wide double doors.

Barlow loved the cozy comfort of the barn. As he entered its dense moist air, he breathed its heady bouquet of manure, straw, and sweaty cowhides. He nodded toward Tom, the big gray farm cat, then ambled to the back of the barn, chatting with neighbors and savoring every pungent moment in the neighborly dirt and straw.

Already Eudora and the other cows were standing in their stalls waiting to be milked. One of the first challenges the animals faced on the dark day that Grover died was how to ease the cows' suffering and save their precious milk. After some quick experimentation, they discovered that the delicate lips of half-grown lambs were the best substitute for human hands. Now every morning, two lambs were employed filling buckets with warm creamy milk. When they were done, the buckets were taken to Gert, who mixed it with eggs and corn, then scooped the gooey paste into bowls and buckets for the dogs and pigs.

Outside the barn, Mara, the largest and most senior of the mares, was pumping water into a large trough on the ground. The old-fashioned hand-pump had proved to be another riddle in those first days. Finally, after various experiments, the cows and horses found that they could raise and lower the handle with their heads—though not without some discomfort to chins and muzzles. They now took daily turns at the pump, filling the common trough for all to share.

As Mara labored this morning, a line of thirsty hens was already perched on its edge, dipping their heads to the slowly rising water.

Still licking his chops from breakfast, Shep squeezed between them and lapped up the cold water with his long pink tongue.

His drink was suddenly interrupted by the clatter of approaching hooves.

A wild-eyed ewe galloped up to the trough and stopped in a cloud of dust.

At last, after several false starts, she managed to gasp out between gulps of air, "A wild. Animal. Has. Taken over. The. Sheep shed. Sound. The war cry. Rally. The troops. We have to defend. The farm!"

CHAPTER 4

Even accounting for the panicky nature of sheep, the other animals were alarmed by the ewe's announcement. Coming so soon after yesterday's pageant, their imaginations were filled with images of giant bears and huddled armies readying for battle. When the animals finally reached the distant shed and caught sight of the invader, they breathed a collective sigh of relief.

"It's only a deer," Barlow said, stepping closer. "Why all the commotion?"

"Only a deer?" said the old ewe. "Only a deer? A WILD deer, you mean. A wild BEAST from the forest, come to steal our food and destroy our way of life."

As the sheep bleated angrily in chorus, Shep edged closer and sniffed at the deer's hind hoof.

"It's the doe who came under the fence yesterday," he said. "She's still bleeding. See, her shoulder has been torn. Claw marks," he added, pointing with his nose. "And big ones, too."

The animals gasped and stepped back at the sight of bloody flesh.

A mare whinnied softly. "There's a mountain lion out there somewhere. In the forest."

A nervous shudder rippled through the crowd.

"Look at the size of those bloody furrows," a hen added. "That must be one big cat."

"Perhaps he will negotiate," Pierre interjected, eyeing the distant fence from his perch on a mare's back. "Cats are highly intelligent creatures. Surely they are amenable to reason. I suggest that we form a diplomatic delegation at once. Perhaps we can convince the lion that it is in his own best interest to avoid contact with the farm. I would lead our diplomatic team myself were my presence not essential here to marshal the ducks and chickens."

"That lion wouldn't dare come here," offered Garth with a toss of his massive head. "They're afraid of human settlements. Besides, I don't think he'd want to face the lot of us. Remember how we drove off that bear?"

"But what about the *deer*?" insisted the indignant ewe. "It's taken over our shed. It's wild. It's dangerous. It's sleeping on our straw! Get it OUT. Get it OUT right now. No wild animals on the farm!"

An approving murmur swept through the crowd.

"No trespassing," someone cackled from the rear.

"Yeah, that's right," a deep voice lowed. "No trespassing."

Gert edged a bit closer and sniffed at the recumbent doe's neck.

"I think it's dead," she said. "Her eyes are closed. She isn't moving."

"No, she's breathing," Shep said. "Just listen." He cocked an ear toward her head. "She's only asleep."

Eudora, the old Guernsey, hobbled by age and arthritis, crept forward at last to examine their unwanted guest.

"She's lost a lot of blood," she concluded. Then after a moment's thought, she added, "The poor dear is harmless, I think."

"Harmless or not," said Bertha, with a quick glance at her mate, "she's got to go. There's only so much food to go around. It's almost winter. Them that don't gather, don't eat."

The herd murmured assent.

"Kit, you're Chief Executive," said Raymond at last, looking up at the giant stallion. "Make her leave the farm at once."

Nudged forward by the company, Kit edged up and reluctantly addressed the deer.

"Sorry, Miss. You've got to leave." He gently prodded her shoulder with a hoof. "You're trespassing. You can't stay here."

The animals gasped as the doe suddenly opened a large brown eye and looked up at the stallion.

"Can't move," she said with a plaintive sigh. "Too tired. From blood loss. Must rest."

Then closing her eyes again, she lay her head down and fell instantly back to sleep.

Kit half-heartedly gave the doe another nudge, but this time she didn't respond.

"What should we do?" asked Gert, an edge of panic rising in her voice. "She can't move. We can't just drag her to the fence and throw her over, can we?"

She looked at the sleeping deer and added more gently, "The poor thing's bleeding."

"Poor *thing*! Poor *thing*!" stammered the indignant ewe. "What about us? She's broken the law. She's taken over our shelter. What next? Are we going to tear down the fences and invite the entire population of the forest into our fields?"

"Do something, Kit," quacked Pierre from atop the mare's back. "Step on her! Smash her to bits! Don't be fooled by that sleeping act. She's a dangerous intruder."

"No," Kit replied with a thoughtful headshake. "It's not up to me. We should bring this before the Council."

"That's right," Shep added. "We can't decide here. Let the law decide.

"Eudora," he said, turning to the wise old cow, "What do you think we should do?"

Eudora contemplated his question for a moment, then gently shook her head.

"I'm not sure," she said. "But this is certainly a matter for the Council. The deer can rest here till we've reached a decision together. We'll meet late this afternoon in the barn after chores.

"Betty," she added, turning to the nearest hen. "Go get Ike. We might need legal counsel."

Then turning to the entire assembly, she said, "We're not wild beasts. We're intelligent domesticated farm animals. We'll decide this in Council tonight, according to law and custom."

CHAPTER 5

It was almost dusk before the Animal Council met in the barn to decide the fate of the deer. The Council was composed of one representative from each of the farm's five "houses." Eudora represented the barn; Barlow the pig shed; Raymond the chicken coop; Mara the stables; and Cora, an old ewe, the sheep shed—the symbolic "house" of the two distant pastures. Kit the stallion presided in his role of Chief Executive, and Ike, an old white ram who lived in a yard by the barn, served as Chief Judge and legal counsel.

Around the five members of the Council, an audience of spectators watched from a gallery of stalls and hay bales. Since the sun had already set, a barn owl, known simply as the Professor, sat on a low beam above the assembly, watching the procedure below with large unblinking eyes.

Emma, the ewe who'd discovered the deer, led the case against allowing the doe to stay.

"She's a wild animal," she began, pacing slowly back and forth with measured strides. "A wild animal who has never known the touch or ways of man." She looked appealingly at her sister sheep. "She's dangerous. Her hooves are sharp and represent a serious threat to those of us who live in the pastures."

From her front row seat, Bertha glanced at her mate on the Council, then added her voice to the sheep's.

"There's no grass left, to speak of, this time of year. That means the deer will be eating hay or oats and who knows what. We can't feed every stray that comes sneaking onto the farm in the dark of night. I'm sorry she's hurt. But that's what comes of living the wild life. They're not like us, those wild ones. They live alone, or in small packs or herds—just a buck and a few does, out there in the wild, trying to get a living from swamp grass. In their whole lives they never know a minute's peace. Less than half will live to maturity. The rest will fall to weather, starvation, disease—or a predator's claws.

"Think of it—the doe's barely old enough to breed, and some cougar has already nearly ripped her throat out. She'll be lucky to live out the night. The only reason she's alive is that she sneaked onto our well-defended farm. She's a gypsy, a tramp, a freeloader. She has no business here among hard-working farm animals. We have to strain and sweat to keep ourselves alive. If we let her stay, others will be sure to follow. Before you know it, the farm will be overrun with deer."

"Hear, hear," a mare's voice called from the back. "If we let her stay, we'll be up to our eyes in deer."

The audience buzzed approval. A few began to stamp their feet on the wooden floor.

After the crowd began to settle, a hen stepped forward in her role of advocate for the deer.

"How much is a deer going to eat?" she asked reasonably, turning to face the crowd. "A single deer. And a badly wounded one, at that. You all act like we've been invaded by a pack of coyotes."

At the mention of coyotes, a nervous shudder rippled through the barn.

"Just look at you," she said, turning back to Cora, the old ewe on the Council. "You have hooves like the doe. You both eat grass. You live in the friendly company of your own kind. You're a herd animal, just like her.

"And you," the hen added suddenly, turning to Emma. "The two of you are practically kin. The doe is kind and retiring—as gentle as a lamb, you might say. You're worried about her pointy hooves? Why, a deer is about as ferocious as a buttercup. We've all seen deer before—stepping delicately across the stream at night, just beyond the fence, with their long slender legs. So graceful and delicate, you'd think they could walk on water. Why, a deer never hurt a fly."

"They jump the fence and eat our grass at night," muttered an old ewe from the rear. "If we didn't run them off, they'd eat the field right down to the roots."

"And what about our vegetable garden?" added Bertha. "If the dogs didn't keep them off, they'd eat their way through that like army ants. They're as bad as groundhogs."

"And the trees," added Moll, who loved nothing more than apples. "They'd strip the bark and kill the whole orchard for the sake of an evening meal."

"They smell funny," added Duke, the big Lab, with a snort. "Wild-like. It breaks my concentration. I couldn't think right, smelling that wild scent all day. It'd throw me off."

"It can't be done," said Gert decisively. "We live by law, and such a thing just can't be. There's wild and there's tame, no in between.

"Besides," she added, brightening, "she can't live here. She hasn't got a name."

"Ahhhh," sighed the audience with approval. And for a moment, the matter seemed settled.

The prosecuting ewe, Emma, nodded toward the crowd as if having clinched the case.

From her place on the Council, Eudora cleared her throat to propose that they take a vote, when suddenly something unprecedented happened. With a flutter of wings, the little barn owl, who'd been perched silently above them throughout the debate, drifted down and lighted on the nearest hay bale. Then he cleared his throat to speak.

"Well, if it's only a matter of a name," he said with a smile toward the Council. "What is a name, but a mere convention? A random term by which we address one another, no more. We can give the deer a name, if it comes to that. I shall do it myself, in fact," he said. "I shall call her *Xena*."

The Professor blinked his large eyes at the Council. Then without so much as a shrug, he turned his head 180 degrees and blinked at the assembly behind him.

"*Xena*?" Gert asked. "What kind of name is that?"

The Professor smiled.

"It means *guest*," he said, puffing his chest. Then as if at his own sagacity, he bobbed his head up and down with a knowing air.

"Guest, huh?" said Duke. "I guess that sounds about right. She is a guest, kind of."

After a moment of puzzled silence, the animals began shifting nervously about. Gert tried to seize the moment and steer the Council back toward a quick resolution.

"Now if you please, let's return to the disposition of the deer. . . ." But before she could finish, a small voice interrupted.

"Don't call her 'the deer.' Her name is Xena."

Gert stopped and stared at the upstart with a look of amazement. It was Emma, the prosecutor, and the deer's first antagonist.

Kit, now acting the role of Chief Executive, turned from the ewe to Eudora and said, "The law says nothing of guests. What is the customary way to treat a guest?"

"Well," the old cow said with a puzzled frown, "we've never had one before. I suppose it's customary to give them lodging and food during their stay. Their brief stay," she added quickly. "That is, if she were actually a guest and not an—"

"She can stay in the shed if she wants," interrupted Emma. "I suppose she is a kind of distant cousin to us sheep. She can stay till she's well enough to go. That is," she quickly corrected, with a bow toward Eudora, "if that's what the Council decides."

Shep, who'd been following the shifting tides of argument, felt suddenly lost. Since the death of their human caretakers, the animals had lived strictly according to their laws, without exception. He appealed to Ike, the wise old ram who served as the ultimate legal authority.

"What about the first law, Ike? No Trespassing."

Ike narrowed his yellow eyes in thought. Then with an uncertain shake of his head, he replied, "I suppose, ahem, we might see this as something less than a strictly legal matter. Though technically we might describe this as a case of trespassing. . . . What are we to do? Kill her or keep her, those are our only options. We can't drive her out. Not now, when she's near death. Rather, we might, as many have suggested, simply regard her as a temporary guest. Ahem.

Then, when she is well, we'll gently but firmly urge the deer to go. Being a wild creature, she will not be confined by fences. Nature will lead her back to the forest, and our problem will resolve itself. Ahem. As long as the sheep don't mind, we'll let her recover there, in the shed. It's the nearest place to the woods anyway."

Though a few animals muttered protests under their breath, Ike's words seemed to settle the matter. The assembly began to break up and drift away to their separate berths. Shep decided that until the matter was settled, he'd visit the distant sheep shed and monitor the deer's recovery. When the time came, he'd make sure the deer left the farm. More than any other animal, the task of guarding the farm's borders fell to him. For now, though, he was content to join his mate on their straw bed at the back of the barn, near Eudora's stall. Shep was unusually tired tonight, and the thought of Jessy's warm back pressed against his gently rising chest filled him with warm contentment and the urge to sleep.

CHAPTER 6

Shep's worries about the deer proved to be unfounded. Despite their initial resistance, the sheep took to nursing the doe like practiced hands. Every day, Emma brought a pail of water from the stream so she could drink. The other sheep brought mouthfuls of grass and other delicacies to nourish her till her strength returned. Within a week, the deer was up on her feet again, grazing and strolling down to the stream to drink. Then one dark moonless night the question of what to do with her was answered when, without a word of good-bye, she slipped from the sheep shed, crossed the stream, and returned to her home in the forest.

For days afterward, the sheep spoke of her with quiet affection, imitating her odd manner of speech and laughing at her quaint mis-understandings. They seemed to take a special delight in repeating her name, especially among the other animals, as if to show off their intimacy with the exotic stranger. The other animals asked about her often, never seeming to tire of the subject of their guest.

"So, did Xena like it here then?" asked Mara. "I suppose she did. Living under a roof; having her food brought to her; being surrounded by so many intelligent, well-meaning friends. I suppose the woods will look pretty bleak now that she's had a taste of farm life."

"No, that Xena was no fool," her sister Moll added. "She knew where to go. No one can say we haven't got a heart, us farm animals."

Then with a smile, she added, "Imagine what she'll say to the rest of her kind out there in the wild."

"Just so she doesn't bring 'em back here," muttered Duke under his breath. "The smell of her spoor makes me crazy like."

"It's not Xena's fault you rolled around in it like a drunken bird in fermenting berries," countered Emma. "Have a little self-control. Nobody makes you act the fool."

"What do you know?" countered Duke, rising to his full height and puffing out his chest. "You couldn't smell bear droppings if you stepped in 'em. All you sheep ever do is stick your face in the grass, oblivious to everything. If Shep and I didn't watch over you, you couldn't find your way to the barn."

With that, the big Lab trotted off toward the pasture to help Shep patrol the fence.

Their guest was soon forgotten as the air turned cold and the animals began preparing for the coming winter. When Raymond, the rooster, informed the Council that the time had come for their winter holiday, a work party of pigs, horses, and dogs was formed to gather the decorations. All afternoon, they trooped back and forth from the farmhouse basement to the barn, dragging boxes and wooden crates.

Gert, for her part, loved this time of year. Holidays brought out the best in the old goose. As the animals discharged their loads in the barn, she fussed about, supervising their placement and arranging things to her taste. The animals not engaged in setting up the crèche chatted quietly in the stalls or among the hay bales. This time of year, even the ducks and geese spent most of their time here, scratching the dirt floor for nonexistent insects and watching the work progress. Mostly, though, they just tried to stay out of the way.

"No, no, no. Put the shepherd here," Gert directed Duke, who gripped the figurine between his jaws like a slain duck. "They're shepherds. They're supposed to be looking over there, toward the manger."

"What's a manger?" the Lab asked, dropping the wooden figure to speak.

"It's the trough, idiot, where the animals eat. Now pick that up and put it over here."

"I thought that's where the baby went," the dog replied.

"Just leave the thinking to me. It's not time for the baby. Now go back to the basement and bring the crate with all the little animals. And tell Kit to get things moving. It'll be dark soon.

"You, there," she shouted at a cow, who had sidled too close to the crèche. "Step back, please. You're going to knock over the wall."

Gert surveyed the confusion, tut-tutting and shaking her head, "Has anybody checked to see if Ike is ready?" she called above the noisy buzz. "We celebrate tomorrow night, you know. Is anyone even listening?"

She threw up her wings in dismay, then discharged her annoyance at a pair of chicks who'd crossed her path, scooting them out of her way with a flap of her great wings.

By nightfall the next day, preparations were complete. As shadows lengthened across the yard, the animals retreated to the friendly confines of the barn, where they gossiped, scratched, and bickered until Ike the old ram appeared in the doorway, signaling the hour had finally come.

After a glance at the tightly packed crowd, Ike turned to the crèche, which suddenly became a magnet of attention.

There was something magical about the miniature barn within the wooden walls of the real barn looming above it. The animals stared at the little figures as if hypnotized, each noting its place in the scene.

Shep glanced over at Jessy and Pip, his mate and pup, then turned and stared at the crèche. Though there were no dogs among its wooden figures, the manger was surrounded by a group of adoring shepherds, who shared his vocation and name. The crooks they carried looked just like the one on the sign above the farm's front gate.

At the sight of the miniature cattle, Eudora and the other cows sighed. The sheep, who always felt underappreciated, noted with smiles that their kind took pride of place, crowding right up to the manger and the child. The ducks, chickens, and geese were utterly dumbstruck by the angels, which were perched atop the roof, spreading golden wings.

At his makeshift podium atop a hay bale, Ike leaned out over the congregation like an ancient prophet. The ram was so old now that his once-white wool had yellowed to the color of old lace. Both Chief Judge and High Priest, Ike used his occasional sermons to share his store of wisdom with the others. It was whispered that he was so old he knew the children of Grover and Evelyn before they left the farm.

Clearing his throat with a loud "Ahem," the old ram beamed down at his congregation, then spoke in clear but gentle tones to the silent crowd.

CHAPTER

"Men did not always stand on two legs," the ram began, "but walked on four, like the other forest animals. His hands were but half formed, like an eagle's claws, and incapable of grasping. His mind could not hold cunning in its net, but like a spider web too finely spun, let thought escape. He lived in the woods like a squirrel, eating nuts and berries, or foraging for roots, or eating carrion like the crow. He was wordless as a stone and knew not the magic of fire.

"Then walking through the forest one day, he met a dog. The dog was hungry and the man drew him close with friendly grunts and fed him a scrap of carrion. The two became friends from that day on and learned to hunt, the dog tracking, the man following and dispatching their prey. They killed and feasted together like a pack of wolves.

"Then one day, while walking through a meadow, they encountered a horse. The man admired its grace and speed and strength. With the help of the dog, he corralled and tamed the beast. Then one day he mounted and rode the horse, sharing its pride and strength, like a lord of the earth.

"While riding one day, he encountered a mother cow. He envied the cow's swollen udders so ripe with milk, so he decided to tame her too and enjoy her bounty. Then he met a sheep and, being cold, he envied her rich warm coat of wool. With the help of his dog, he trapped and tamed the sheep. He protected her from prowlers that lurked near the flock and kept her safe from harm. When her coat was thick, he trimmed it to make a shield against the wind.

"But still the man was wild and rootless as a wolf, lacking even a burrow in which to rest his head. He killed and ate live flesh and drank hot blood. He growled and snarled and made sounds without meaning.

"Then one night in a dream, a man-shepherd came to him with visions from another world. With spirit-force, he tamed the man as the man had tamed the beasts. As the man slept, the man-shepherd filled his mind with words and instructed him how to gather wood and make fire. Then when the man awoke, the man-shepherd led him from the forest to a meadow and there taught him how to fashion the first ax. With the ax, the man cut down trees and made a house. With stones, he made a hearth to cook his food. Then he chopped down the trees and fashioned them into rails and fenced in the meadow to keep out those beyond.

"The man said, 'Within this fence shall live the gentle and wise animals I have tamed. Outside it shall live the beasts who feast on flesh and know not the comfort of roofs or the warmth of fire.' Then, to separate the tame from the wild, he wrote his first words and held them up to the forest:

"NO TRESPASSING.

"From that day forth, those words became our first law and commandment.

"Thus man and his domestic companions lived in warmth and comfort, sharing their lives and labors. As the man-shepherd had taught him, the man taught the animals speech, saying, '*Whoa, giddyup, stay, come, good boy, woo pig, easy there.*' As the days passed, the animals grew in understanding, becoming more man-like in their thoughts and habits. As the animals lived in safety and harmony, they learned gentleness and peace.

"Then one night, as he had once visited the man, the spirit-shepherd visited a wise old ram in his sleep and gave him counsel. When the ram awoke, he recorded the secret knowledge with carved symbols. First he etched into the wall for all to see, NO TRESPASSING, then

"'WALK BY DAY, NOT BY NIGHT,' the second commandment.

"'DO NOT KILL OR EAT LIVING FLESH,' said the third.

"The fourth and final command was, 'WALK IN THE WAYS OF MAN.'"

Having delivered these, the old ram gathered the domestic herds around him and spoke the following words of prophecy.

"Like men who walk on two legs and work with hands, we animals have grown in the ways of wisdom. In domesticity we have learned to value concord over discord and tameness over savagery. Hearing men speak, we have learned to grasp the meanings of shaped sounds. Our spirits have grown larger and more complex and multifarious. We know joy and sorrow, loyalty and gratitude, work and service. Having names and a perception of the good, we walk each day down the path to personhood.

"The same spirit-shepherd that tamed the wildness out of man has spoken to me and given me a promise. He said that a day will come when the spirit will put on flesh and come to us in the guise of a human infant. Born in a barn, he will sleep in a humble manger. He will draw men and animals to him on an equal footing. Men will crouch down on all fours, like cattle; and beasts will speak together like men, each in its tongue. The holy spirit-child will love all living creatures. The line between man and beast will melt away.

"Men will sprout golden wings, like those of geese, and perch on the roof and sing like meadow larks. Shepherd and sheep will come together as one flock. From the lamb, men will learn humility and meekness; from man, sheep draw cunning and resolve. All wildness will be driven from the earth, and the lion and bear will be gentle like the lamb."

Ike directed the congregation toward the manger.

"Look at the creatures standing there before you. See there, on the roof arrayed like birds, the geese-men. Half men, half birds, they are, with golden wings. Joined, they are, flesh and spirit, in one body. Their voices resound like geese passing overhead. They sing of hope and of the coming shepherd child."

As Ike paused, the animals gazed at the nativity scene in wide-eyed wonder. There in the manger lay the infant Ike described, surrounded by men and beasts on the straw-covered floor.

"Hallelujah," cried an old goose. "Praise the spirit-shepherd."

Her ecstatic cry was echoed by a ewe.

Then the old ram leaned forward and concluded his sermon with these words:

"Follow the law. Allow no trespass. 'Do Not Kill.' When wildness threatens, stand shoulder to shoulder and preserve our precious farm."

CHAPTER 8

Six weeks of frost and sleet followed Ike's holiday sermon. Then daffodils poked green shoots through the loamy soil, signaling the onset of spring, and the long hot season of plowing and planting began. For weeks the animals spent every waking moment in arduous labor.

Summer brought the first fruit of the orchards—peaches and cherries. The pigs and horses especially loved the fruit, but lacking hands, could reap only a portion of it. Being the tallest, the horses picked the lowest hanging peaches, then shook the branches to send more thudding to the ground for the pigs to gather. The cherries, though, were too high for even these inefficient tactics, so all the animals could do was look and lick their lips.

"It's a pity the blackbirds will get those cherries," sighed Barlow. "What I wouldn't give to have a bucket of those little jewels for breakfast, all covered in milk."

"Yes," sighed his mate. "If I ever catch one of those blackbirds, I'll chew him into inky paste."

"No use crying over spilled milk," Duke chipped in. "I just wish those thieving varmints walked on the ground. Then we'd see how they'd steal our food and fly off, waving feathers in my face."

All the animals nodded in silent agreement.

And so it was with total astonishment that the pigs woke the next morning to a bucket of fresh-picked cherries.

After greedily devouring them, the pigs trotted about the farm, inquiring where they'd come from and how they'd been miraculously picked.

Outside the barn, their astonishment increased when they met a crowd staring at a pyramid of baskets filled with fruit.

"Where'd they come from?" a mare asked, stepping close to sniff. "We horses were asleep in the pasture. How did these get picked?"

"Wasn't us," replied Gert, craning her long neck to inspect the dust for evidence. "Look here. In the dirt. It looks like little footprints."

Looking where the goose pointed, the mares drew back in astonishment.

"They're little *hands*!" observed May.

"Move over," Duke muttered, edging forward. "Let me have a sniff at that."

"Can't be handprints," clucked a hen. "They're too small. Look there. It's like a tiny little foot."

"A *human* foot," added a ewe, and the crowd took a small step backward.

Raising his head, Duke said, "Don't recognize the smell." He cleared his nostrils with a loud sniff. "Don't know what it is, but it certainly ain't human.

"Go fetch Shep," he said, turning to Gert. "He knows every smell there is."

Till Shep arrived, the animals speculated about what sort of miracle they'd witnessed. Perhaps, said some, Ike's prophecy had come true. Perhaps somewhere on the farm a tiny hybrid creature—half man, half beast—had visited them in fulfillment of prophecy.

After sniffing the print, Shep stepped back and shook his head.

"I don't recognize the smell either," he said. "But one thing I do know: the creature isn't human. Whatever it is, it's wild."

"*Wild?*" shouted Pierre, with a flutter of wings. "Wild? The creature must immediately be tracked down and exterminated. We can't have a savage beast sneaking about the farm."

"He brought us cherries," Bertha sulked. "A whole bucket of 'em. Over there, inside our pen, when we woke up."

"How on earth did the creature pick them?" wondered Moll, raising an eye toward the cherry tree. "Even the lowest branches are far beyond my reach."

She furrowed her brow in thoughtful concentration.

"Whatever it is," she said, eyeing the brimming baskets, "I hope we can learn its methods."

"Learn its methods?" shouted Pierre. "What are you talking about? We must track the creature down and kill it immediately."

"Shep," the duck called, turning to the dogs. "You and Duke must form two search parties. I will not sleep until the creature has been driven from the farm.

"Ladies," he called to his web-footed mates, "We must go to the pond and plan our offensive strategy. Till then, we will await the outcome of Shep's reconnaissance."

Turning abruptly, the duck marched off toward the distant pond, leaving Shep and Duke to organize search parties.

Once a posse had been formed, Shep lowered his nose to the ground and led it across the barnyard to the cherry tree. From there he tracked the creature's scent across the barnyard till they approached the chicken coop.

"It's in the coop, in the coop," honked Gert, emerging from the door and racing toward them. "Duke and Raymond have it cornered."

Shep dashed into the henhouse and joined the defenders circled across the room.

"Come out of that corner," growled Duke, "or I'll break your neck. It's only a matter of time before we get you."

"Get out at once," demanded Raymond, puffing himself to twice his normal size. "Or I'll slash your face to ribbons and peck out your eyes."

Despite the threats, the little creature kept his back tightly wedged into the corner, baring his dagger teeth in defiance.

The coop was now so crowded with spectators that Shep could barely creep up to the standoff beside Duke.

"Surrender peacefully," he said, pushing past the Lab, "and we'll escort you safely to the fence and let you go. Resist, and you won't leave this coop alive."

A black mask covered the creature's wildly darting eyes. He had the look of a bandit caught red-handed.

"What is it?" shouted a hen, in near hysteria. "It's not a dog. It's not a possum. It's bigger than Raymond. If Duke hadn't come, we'd none of us be alive."

"Calm down," said Kit, poking his big head in the doorway. "I've seen one of those before, beyond the fence. He's not so big. If he comes out, I could crush him with one hoof."

"No need, no need for that," hissed the creature through bared teeth. "I come in peace. I mean none of you harm."

Then, as if to show his good intentions, he reached out in a gesture of goodwill.

The crowd gasped and took a step backward toward the door.

"Why, look!" cried Gert. "The creature . . . it has *hands*!"

Excited squawks and whinnies almost drowned out the captive's reply.

"'Course I got hands," he said. "I'm a raccoon." He smiled crookedly. "What do you think I used to pick those cherries?"

He flexed his fingers, to enhance the odd effect they had on his captors.

"The name's Rags," he said. "Looks to me like you could use my help.

"If you'll just back off and give me some breathing room, maybe we can get to know each other. To tell the truth, I could use some conversation. Not to mention a safe place to cool my heels. Try living out there in the woods sometime, dodging hungry bobcats and coyotes. I'm not getting any younger. Truth is, I've lost a step or two— and out there, that can be fatal.

"Still," he added more brightly, "there's a lot of picking left in these old hands. If you don't break my neck, big fella, I could teach you all a thing or two about picking. Those trees are full of fruit. We can work out something to our mutual advantage. Don't kill the golden goose, as the saying goes."

CHAPTER 9

A decision as grave as deciding the fate of the raccoon could only be made by the Council. As in the case of Xena, the wounded deer, two factions formed to debate the raccoon's case. The pigs and horses, who wanted a helpful ally in the orchards, argued the benefits of letting the raccoon stay. The chickens and ducks, fearing the creature's size and secret intentions, stood firmly behind the law that said no wild creatures could live on the farm.

"Think of all that fruit," Barlow argued. "We could dry it out in the sun and store it for winter. I, for one, wouldn't mind something sweet and juicy to brighten our winter fare. Even if you don't eat fruit, think how those of us who do would eat less of the other things you like, leaving more for everyone. What's the harm of letting the poor little critter stay here and help us work the farm?"

Emma, the old ewe who'd befriended Xena, pointed out another benefit of letting the raccoon stay.

"Those little hands would sure do a better job of milking than what young lambs can manage," she said with a smart look. "You try milking those big udders with only your lips—without drinking or spilling half. We sheep are tired of working our poor jaws stiff for you pigs and dogs. Rags could get the milking done before ol' Barlow half finished gathering the eggs."

"But, but, but," sputtered Hetty, the senior hen, "the creature is dangerous. It was our coop he invaded, after all. What do you think he was doing there, picking cherries? He'd come to eat our chicks and steal our eggs. I don't want to live the rest of my life in terror, thank you very much. It's fine for you fat pigs to have him around to help you stuff your faces. What harm can he do to you? It's us chickens who'll pay in blood if the raccoon stays."

"It's not like keeping the deer," Shep chipped in, rising to his feet. "Her stay was only temporary. We could hardly turn her away. She was near death. But this big fella's wild, and he means to stay. He'd leave his wild smell all over the place, making it hard for me to do my job of sniffing out invaders. Ask Duke, he'll tell you too. We can't keep a raccoon on the farm, no matter how helpful."

"It's simply a matter of the law," Eudora said firmly. "There's wild and there's tame. The raccoon's wild. He simply cannot stay."

"Ike," called the cow, addressing the old ram, "you have to tell them plain and simple. The law is clear. Only domestic animals can live on the farm."

The old ram nodded, almost sadly. "It's true," he said. "The, ahem, raccoon is wild. That's clear. No telling how he'd act among us peaceful domestics. Eudora's right. The law says it plain and true: 'No Trespassing.' There's no way to misinterpret that."

A murmur of protest arose from the pigs and horses. Barlow stepped forward again to bolster their case.

"If you stop and think about it, the raccoon's not really wild. He already has a name. And just look at those hands! It's like Ike said in his sermon. It's prophecy come true. He walks in the ways of man. Could there be a clearer sign than that? The wild and tame joined together? Surely the law does not intend for us to exclude our spiritual brothers."

Now the geese and chickens squawked back in angry rebuttal.

"Take a good look at those spiritual teeth of his," Hetty snapped, speaking for the hens. "They're egg crackers, they are. Made for cracking wings and necks, too. Nothing else."

"Why *that* remark," said a cool voice from above, "is nothing but the crudest form of xenophobia."

A flutter of feathers overhead signaled the presence of the barn owl. As all eyes turned upward, the gray Professor stretched his wings and slowly descended toward the assembly, stopping to perch on a stall.

For an instant the animals were too flummoxed to reply. Then scratching a floppy ear, Duke stepped forward to ask the question on every tongue.

"Xena-phobia?" he asked. "What the heck is *that*?"

The little owl smiled, blinking fathomless dark eyes.

"That, my friend, is a very terrible thing. And it's *Xeno*phobia, by the way. It means 'fear of strangers.' A disabling illness affecting little minds."

None of the animals had the slightest idea what the owl was talking about. Fear of strangers seemed to them the most fundamental form of self-defense. What had them puzzled was the word itself, which sounded, as Duke had heard it, like the name of their old friend, the doe. No one wanted to seem inhospitable to that poor wounded creature. Then, too, it was such a very long and formidable word. It sounded terrible, like a mind-infecting virus. No one wanted to admit to harboring such a terrible thing as that.

Suddenly, the thought of accepting the raccoon into their society seemed preferable to being accused of infection by this frightening disease.

"Well, no, I didn't mean to be xenaphobic," stuttered the old hen, unconsciously mispronouncing the new word. "I was just saying that, you know, it might not be such a good thing to have a wild creature lurking about the farm. I certainly didn't mean to sound xenaphobic."

"Perhaps," said the owl, "you meant to put it another way. Perhaps what you really meant to say was that the distinction between wild and tame is an illusory construct. What, after all, defines tameness but living in domestic comity on a farm? What defines wildness but the failure to live in such a state of peace? If the nominally wild comes to live in a state of tameness, then does he not by definition become tame?"

The little owl smiled with his eyes.

"Of course, you're not xenophobic," he tut-tutted to the hen. "You've simply fallen prey to binary thinking. Such dualism is symptomatic of our conditioning. A simplistic construct easily cast aside."

"I see what the Professor is saying," interrupted Barlow, who was nearly as quick-witted as Shep. "What the Professor is saying is that if we make Rags a citizen of the farm and he follows the same laws as us, then he won't be wild anymore. He'll be tame."

The pig smiled at his own compelling logic. The other animals stared at him blankly, as if suddenly pacified.

"What about it?" asked Kit, who dearly loved his apples. The prospect of an unending supply stirred his normally silent tongue.

"If Rags agrees to become a member of the farm and follow our laws, I say we tame him just like we were tamed. Who knows? In time, we might erase wildness from the whole world, the way Ike said.

"And besides, it'll sure be fine having apples next winter, even dried."

A murmur of approval from the horses drowned out the muttered protests of the hens. Before a voice could raise another objection, Ike addressed the raccoon from his judge's seat.

"Step forward, Mr. Rags. If you'll agree to be instructed in our ways, we will teach you the path of tameness. If you are willing to be tutored by one of our elders and closely examined by the Council, we will meet back here in seven days and put you to the test."

The raccoon stepped forward to face the Council with beaming countenance.

"I'd be honored, sir," he said, "to live here and become tame like all of you. It's high time I settled down. I'm a quiet sort of fellow, really. I'm tired of living one step ahead of a bobcat's belly. Why, you couldn't get me to go back into that forest for all the berries in the world."

He turned to the hens and sheep. "When you see how hard I work, I'll make you glad you took me in. You'll never regret your decision, I promise you that."

On Ike's orders, Gertrude accepted the job of instructing the would-be citizen. The animals all agreed that there was no creature more suitable than the old goose to civilize the raccoon. She loved the farm and revered its laws and customs.

For her part, Gert was glad to take the job. She practically glowed at the prospect of transforming the wild raccoon into a model citizen. The whole farm would benefit from the creature's transformation. When she was done, those little hands would serve the higher good of Green Pastures Farm. Her fellow citizens would all thank her for accomplishing the task.

CHAPTER 10

The first thing that Gertrude discovered about the raccoon was that he seemed to be as smart as any animal on the farm. In a fraction of the time it took the chickens and sheep, he had memorized the four commandments.

"Got 'em," said the raccoon after a single lesson. "No Trespassing. 'Walk by Day, Not by Night.' 'Do Not Kill.' 'Walk in the Ways of Man.'"

The raccoon smiled proudly.

Gertrude wondered if deep down the creature wasn't half tame already. Those hands of his were a powerful argument in his favor.

"Very good," the goose said. "You understand, of course, what the words imply. Take 'Do Not Kill,' for example. It might mean certain dietary restrictions."

She gave the raccoon a penetrating stare.

"Oh, I see what you mean. No worries there. I can live just fine off insects and berries. And the occasional bit of grain. And mice, of course—if such a thing's permitted."

Gertrude thought a moment. The farm cats, Tom and Calley, were dedicated mousers. They kept the farm from being overrun by rodents who'd eat every bit of grain if given the chance.

"No, eating mice is permitted," she said. "They're only vermin, the better done with. The law applies strictly to farm animals, not thieving rodents. No one will object if you destroy a mouse.

"Now step over here and take at look at this tablet."

The raccoon complied, looking up and eyeing the symbols scratched onto the barn's wooden wall.

Gertrude cleared her throat and pointed toward an awkwardly drawn symbol, then said in her most impressive teacher's voice, "The first sign means, 'Many animals, one farm.' Can you repeat that?"

"Sure. Many animals, one farm," said the raccoon. "What's the next one there, beside it?"

"Just a minute," Gertrude said. "Not so fast. It's not the words that count, but the idea. A farm is made up of many different species. Birds. Canines. Swine. Cattle. Horses. By nature, each wants to associate with its kind. It first looks out for its own individual interest, and then the interest of its species.

"But on a farm, we have to look past ourselves. We have to learn to consider the interest of others.

"Of course, each species has its own special strengths and weaknesses. Chickens can't frighten off intruders. But dogs can't lay eggs. Geese can't carry heavy buckets, but pigs don't honk at strangers. See what I mean?"

The raccoon nodded. "Like picking apples," he said with a broad smile.

"That's right," continued the goose. "Individually, we each have our own strengths, but together, we are something larger and more powerful. Separately, our survival is uncertain; as a farm, though, we are powerful—and one."

Sometimes when delivering such speeches, Gertrude got so choked up she could barely speak.

"Ah-honk," she said, clearing her nostrils.

"Now that next symbol," she said, craning her neck over her shoulder, "is meant to show that all of us walk on the same level ground. There's a little rhyme I used to teach the sheep, which goes like this:

"*Hoof, web, paw, claw—on level ground, under one law.*"

Gertrude smiled. "That means no matter how big or small, how fierce or timid, how smart or slow an animal might be, it's equal to every other on the farm. A mighty stallion like Kit or a whip-smart dog like Shep gets the same treatment as the shyest sheep or the dimmest hen in the henhouse."

The raccoon smiled, then repeated Gertrude's rhyme in sing-song, word for word.

It was almost frightening how quickly Rags caught on.

"The last symbol there," she said, pointing with her bill, "is an ear and a tongue, overlapping. It means every animal has an equal voice and can say whatever he wants, without fear of retribution. The ear means we all have the right—and the obligation—to listen. You've seen the way we work things out in the Council. The Council members are the voices of the farm's five houses. When you become a citizen, you'll be assigned a house to represent you too, so you can have a say and a vote on important issues that affect us.

"And of course," concluded Gert, "there's the sign on top.

"NO TRESPASSING.

"It means two very important things.

"First, as a commandment, it means to follow the path of tameness and be good. As a law, it means guard the farm's borders, drive off intruders, and keep the fences strong. You'll understand all this, if you keep your eyes and ears open. Watch Shep. He's the living, breathing meaning of those words. There's not much that gets past him."

Over the next few days, Rags followed Gert's advice and learned the ways of the farm. He was a model worker, rising early to milk the cows, then marching off to pick fruit in the orchard. The pigs and horses were growing plump and sleek from his efforts there.

As Gert had expected, the examination before the Council was swift and successful. When Ike announced that Rags had passed his citizenship test, the animals applauded wildly. Then Gertrude led the raccoon in his oath and the others pounded his back, congratulating him on becoming a citizen.

After modestly accepting their good wishes, Rags inquired which of the five houses would be his home.

"Well, you don't actually have to live in the house to be a member. For practical purposes, you could live almost anywhere," explained a hen. "For instance, the ducks spend most of their time at the pond, but they're assigned, for the sake of voting, to the barn. Most of us spend a good deal of time in the barnyard, just hanging about the water trough or passing the day. You can pretty much live wherever you want—if it's okay with the current residents."

Despite their initial enthusiasm over Rags becoming a citizen, no one was particularly keen to have him join their house.

As for the raccoon, he didn't want to live in the distant pastures with the sheep and cattle, so after a bit of thought, he decided to bed down in the big cherry tree—at least for the summer, then move indoors to an empty shed when it got cold. For voting purposes, he was added to the barn, a compromise that seemed to satisfy everyone.

Naturally, when the time came for picking apples, the animals turned to Rags to lead the effort. But on the first misty morning of harvest time, the raccoon couldn't be found.

Finally, Duke tracked him down in a corner of the barn, where he was curled up in a ball, quietly moaning.

"What's the matter?" asked Eudora, leaning down. "Are you sick?"

"No," moaned the raccoon. "I'm not, I'm just terribly lonely. I miss my mate and son, back in the woods."

The news of the raccoon's stress—and of his family status—spread quickly across the farm. Soon the horses and cows came trotting up to inquire about his state of mind. Those apples were ready to harvest and they were eager to have a taste.

"So you miss your mate and little one," said Eudora, nodding kindly. She understood the pain of separation, having lost a calf.

"If only I could bring them here, to safety," Rags lamented. "The bears are coming down to the valleys this time of year. And ever since the other farms went under, the coyotes have gotten bolder and more reckless. I worry about my kin. My son's only half grown, the sole survivor of our litter. I think it would be best if I went back. It was foolish of me to think I could live here in safety while they fended for themselves."

The raccoon blew his nose and wiped his teary eyes.

"Unless, of course," he stammered, "but, no, that wouldn't be right. . . . That wouldn't be right."

"What?" asked Moll. "What wouldn't be right?"

The raccoon sighed piteously.

"No, it's too much. It isn't fair to ask."

"Ask what?" asked Bertha and Barlow almost in unison. "What wouldn't be fair?"

"No, no, no. You've been too kind already. I just can't bear to bring myself—" The raccoon broke off in another wrenching sob.

At last they wheedled the information from him. Rags wanted his mate and son, who were living in a hollow tree beyond the fence, to come and join him on the farm.

"Of course, it would only be if you allowed it," he said softly. "And they'd naturally have to become citizens, like me."

"I knew it," muttered a duck under her breath. "First one, then a forest-full of wild ones."

"Well," said Gert, suddenly brightening at the prospect, "they would have to undergo the same citizenship training."

Barlow stepped up and nudged Rags with his snout.

"Look at what a fine citizen Rags turned out to be," the pig said. "None better. Imagine two more sets of hands like that."

He lifted up a black paw with his mouth.

Edging forward, the horses eagerly joined in the raccoon's praise.

"Yes, if Rags is an example of his kind, I say let's bring in the whole family. The more the merrier. Just look at the blisters on that little hand if you don't think he pulls his weight."

"Why, he's as tame as I am," insisted Bertha, edging closer. "He works harder than any of us. I say let's put it to a vote. We could use more pickers like our friend Rags here.

"Eudora," she added, turning to the cow, "call the Council together. This matter requires our immediate attention."

"What about his family?" inquired a ewe. "Will they be safe till then? I'd hate to have something happen while we're deciding."

"Sure, I know right where they are," replied the raccoon, suddenly brightening. "Say the word, and I'll go and fetch them just like that."

"I could accompany him to the fence," volunteered Kit. "And stand guard to make sure nothing happens till he finds his mate."

"I'll be so quick, you won't even know I've gone," said Rags, then quietly added with a smile, "Imagine when they see me living here."

CHAPTER 11

Mrs. Rags and Little Rags, as they came to be called, were rescued from their peril in the forest by Rags and a posse of geese and dogs. The two wild raccoons were at first terrified by the pack of farm animals bearing down on them, but their terror turned to joy when they saw Rags and realized that the others were his friends and allies. The raccoons were escorted safely back to the farm and presented with the delightful prospect of taking up residence. The farm animals quickly befriended the shy but grateful raccoons. By their examples, they taught them how to behave like domestic farm animals and encouraged them to readjust their habits. The two raccoons quickly adapted to their new life and, after a short period of citizenship training under Gertrude, took their oaths and became full-fledged citizens of the farm.

With the addition of two more pairs of hands, the animals reaped a record harvest of cherries and apples. But after two weeks of unremitting labor, the raccoons' fingers became so sore and blistered they could no longer endure picking fruit. Little Rags, the youngster, was relieved of the task for the summer and given the chore of milking cows instead. The horses sighed at the sight of so many unpicked apples, but with a harvest beyond their wildest dreams already stored, they didn't press the issue. All that Kit and the mares could talk about on hot summer afternoons now was the prospect of dried apples in winter.

The three dogs, Shep, Jessy, and Duke, were less enthusiastic about the presence of the raccoons, but they soon grew accustomed to their gamy scent. As they patrolled the fence and fields, they learned to distinguish the pungent scent of raccoon from others that crossed a corner of the farm.

One dark moonless night, a small furry creature left the shadows and, to mask its scent, followed a set of footprints to the orchard, where it climbed a tree and feasted on over-ripe apples until nearly dawn.

This first invasion was so successful, he repeated it every night for the next week.

One morning, though, his greed got the better of his judgment and he stayed till the eastern horizon was turning pink.

As he sat beneath a gnarled apple tree, a pair of powerful paws closed round his neck.

"What are you doing here?" demanded Rags, nearly lifting the little creature off its feet.

"Whoa, whoa, there, big fella. I didn't mean any harm. Let go of my neck, and I'll skedaddle right out of here."

Rags studied the intruder, tightening his grip.

"What are you doing here?" he repeated.

"What does it look like I'm doing? I'm keeping these apples from going to waste."

"You got a name?" asked the raccoon, eyeing him sternly.

"Sure I got a name. Possum. O. Possum. Folks call me Oliver. Or, sometimes, just Big O."

The possum smiled, displaying rows of needle teeth.

"Well, Oliver, you don't look so big to me. Mind explaining what you're up to?"

"Just having a little snack, that's all. I was about to move over there, to that cherry tree. Those cherries are over-ripe and rotting on their stems. Now be a sport and let go of my neck."

Rags gave a scornful snort. "I oughta turn you over to the dogs. They'll make short work of you."

The possum cringed. "Now why would you go and do that?" he asked. "I'm just doing what any creature'd do under the circumstances—trying to survive. Have a heart, friend. Don't call the dogs on me."

Rags released his grip but kept an eye on the intruder.

"There you go," said the possum. "That's better. You think I like having to sneak around like this? We're not all as lucky as you. I've got a missus out there in the woods myself—with a pouch full of little 'uns waiting to make their way into this unforgiving world. How'd you like to be in my situation again, eh? Clinging to life by a thread and hoping your luck don't run out?"

"All right," said Rags. "I'll let you go this time. But you're on your own after that. Better get moving before the rest wake up."

"Get going? Sure," said the possum. "First thing. Just let me take a few of those cherries back for the missus and I'll be on my way. Don't mind me. Get on with your comfortable life. Forget I exist. You won't see me again around these parts. No, sir." And with that, the possum scurried across the yard into the shadows.

Two days later, though, Rags was chagrined to see the possum up to his old tricks. He spotted the little thief carrying a basket of cherries to the pigpen. Inside, Bertha and Barlow were already feasting on an earlier delivery.

The possum spied Rags approaching and waddled away toward the distant fence.

"Hey, it worked for you," he called over his shoulder. "Live and learn's my motto. Heh heh. Thanks for the lesson, friend."

Rags frowned and kicked the dirt. It was time that impudent little fellow was taught a lesson.

The very next morning his wish came true when the farm awoke to furious honking. Gertrude had the possum pinned against the barn and was frantically calling for help.

"Back off, sister," hissed the possum through razor teeth. "Back off or I swear I'll wring your scrawny neck."

Too late for that, thought Rags, as Jessy bounded across the barnyard toward the action. Within seconds, a small army of hens and cows surrounded the intruder.

"Stay back, stay back," shouted the cornered possum. "Stay back, or you'll give me no choice but to . . ."

He grasped his chest with both front paws and began to stagger. "Oh, Oh . . . my heart!"

Jessy stopped growling and recoiled as the possum staggered forward, reeling toward the ground.

"Oh heavens," the possum moaned, "I'm done for, done for—" and collapsed in a lifeless heap, tongue lolling grotesquely from his mouth.

"He's dead," gasped Gertrude. "We frightened the poor little thing to death."

"Served him right," muttered Raymond, dragging his spur across the dirt. "If we hadn't, I'd have had to slit his throat."

Eudora sidled up to the possum and bent an ear toward his chest.

"He's not breathing," she announced. "And, oh dear, he already smells like death."

The animals gasped and recoiled from the dead possum. Living sheltered lives, they had an instinctive terror of death.

"Wait a minute," said Duke, stepping forward and examining the possum more carefully. "He's not dead. I can hear him breathing."

The big Lab poked the motionless possum with his muzzle. At first the possum didn't stir, but after a second push that shifted his head, he reflexively returned to his attitude of gape-jawed death.

"He's faking!" shouted a hen. "The little thief is faking! Kill him, Duke. Right now, bite him before he attacks."

"Attacks?" replied the possum, sitting up with a look of real surprise. "It's *you* who are about to attack *me*.

"All right, then," he said throwing up his paws, "I give up. Resume your attack. Go ahead and kill me. . . . Though I only came to lend you a helping hand."

The possum pointed toward the distant orchard. "Those raccoons have left half your fruit in the trees. Forgive me, but I couldn't bear to see it going to waste."

This remark took the animals by surprise. Before they could gather their wits to challenge him, the possum resumed his friendly patter.

"Don't get me wrong now. You're good animals. Kind and friendly. You deserve the prosperity you enjoy here on your farm. You're a fine, honest, hard-working lot—no one can deny it. That's why I think it's unfair that you have to miss out on all that fruit—just because certain animals don't think enough of you to finish the job.

"Forgive me, but I just couldn't bear it. Those of us lucky enough to be born with two hands . . ." The possum extended his two front paws and wiggled his little fingers.

"As I say, those fortunate enough to be born with hands have an obligation to help the less fortunate. The less, well, naturally endowed," he added with a modest smile.

Stunned by the sight of those wriggling fingers, his captors stood dumbstruck.

"Now I'm not presumptuous enough to ask to be admitted here as a full citizen like some folk. No, sir. Though I might live in the forest, I know my place. Still, we're all intelligent animals. We know that violence is not the answer to this situation. Let me propose, then, a different solution, one that will perhaps work to our mutual advantage.

"Now I don't presume to tell you how to run the farm. You are, as I said, wise and industrious creatures, a model to us all. But here's an idea to consider," he said, finally pausing to take a breath.

"You want those apples down, right? And I want but the tiniest part of them to hold off hunger for me and my family. Instead of making a permanent nuisance of myself, let me ask you to regard me simply as a guest—a temporary guest. A very useful one, perhaps, but only that—a kind of temporary worker.

"Soon as the harvest's done," he added quickly, "I'll leave the farm and return to my home in the forest. So what do you say? Look at these fine digits. They're dying to have a go at that fruit. Just let me do you a friendly service and come fall, you'll never lay your eyes on me again."

CHAPTER 12

When the Council met, the debate over letting the possum stay was hot and heavy, with the pigs, horses, and cows supporting the idea and the dogs, chickens, and sheep opposing it. The possum turned the tide by reminding them that as a non-citizen, he wasn't obliged to work by day, but could follow his own nocturnal habits and pick fruit while the others slept at night.

"I won't be breaking any laws," said the possum, "and I wouldn't get in your way. I'd live here virtually unnoticed, and before you know it, I'll be gone."

Barlow weighed in on the possum's behalf. "He can climb like the raccoons," he said, "snip stems with his teeth, and gather the fruit almost as well as Rags. Now that *Little* Rags is milking cows, we'll be a picker short when the next big crop comes in. Besides, with their hands so sore and blistered, the raccoons can't pick fruit anyway. It's just going to waste. What's the harm in letting one little possum sleep in the wood-pile and pick the fruit by night?" he asked over murmurs of disapproval.

"That's true," added the possum, piping in. "I won't deprive you of food since I'll be eating fruit that will otherwise go to rot. And besides, I also eat insects and mice, which destroy your crops and steal from your grain bins. You're getting two benefits in one."

Despite such reasoning, two of the farm's five legislative houses—the barn and chicken coop—voted against granting the possum temporary status. But the other three houses—the pasture, pigpen, and stables—voted for him to stay. Eudora appealed to Ike to overturn the vote, arguing that letting the possum stay violated their first law, but the old ram waved her off.

"I'm a judge, not a legislative body. If the majority votes to let the possum stay, it's not my place to declare the act illegal. Law says No Trespassing. Well, if we grant permission to one wee creature to work here on a temporary basis, it's not trespassing, is it? He's not a trespasser, but an invited guest."

The decision was greeted by happy oinks and whinnies, and Oliver Possum became the farm's first temporary guest worker.

The day after the decision, the farm awoke to four full baskets of fruit outside the barn, which were immediately dragged off and devoured by the pigs.

The animals spent the next several days preparing for the hardest job of the year: harvesting a hundred acres of corn. The stalks stood higher than a horse's ear and were heavy with ripe green husks.

After Oliver's first harvest of apples, his nightly productivity dropped off, first to three, then two, then one half-filled basket. The horses were beginning to grumble about how little fruit made it past the pigs when his productivity suddenly took an upward turn.

Instead of one basket, they found five at the stable door when they awoke. Then one evening a little past dusk as they were ambling toward the barn, they made a discovery that solved the mystery.

"Quick, come here," whinnied May. "Come see what I've just found."

Kit trotted up and looked where May was staring, then blinked his eyes to correct his faulty vision.

At his feet stood a fat little possum covered with squirming miniature possums a tenth its size. They clutched the large one's fur, burdening it so heavily that the poor thing could barely crawl.

"What's happening?" asked Kit. "Are the little ones eating the big one?"

May smiled. "No, silly. It's a mother possum carrying her young. They're almost too big to ride her anymore. She must be a very patient mother."

"Patient? You have no idea, my lady," said the possum, looking up. "Imagine trotting about the field with sixteen colts clinging to your hide. It'll wear you out, I'll tell you.

"Get off there," she commanded the one clinging to her neck. "Get down. There's no use carting you anymore, the jig is up."

"What are you doing here?" asked Kit, turning suspicious. "You're not supposed to be here. You're trespassing. I don't know whether I should stomp you now or call the dogs and have them tear you apart."

"Oh dear, not that," squealed the possum in horror. "Have some mercy. I'm not trespassing. I'm here on legitimate business."

The horses had no idea what the possum meant by that, but held off crushing her till she explained herself more clearly.

"You see, it's my mate Oliver," the possum explained. "The poor fellow worked so hard picking your fruit that his fingers got all stiff and cramped. You don't think a single possum can pick four baskets of apples every night, do you? That'd sure be a miracle. So I says to him, 'Look, Oliver, let me come over there at night and give you a little help. The little ones are nearly grown now, they can lend a hand too.'

"Before you know it, we're all picking apples by moonlight, and poor Oliver's hands are cured of the cramp.

"Here," she added, reaching into her pouch. "Here's some fine, fresh-picked cherries I brought out here for you."

She reached toward the horses' mouths, shaking a fistful of cherries by the stems.

"I'm Olive," the possum said as they bent down to her treat.

"These here are my kids. You can thank them for some of those apples you ate this morning.

"This here's Olga, and this is Opal. That's Otto, Owen, Otis, Oswald, there. That's Ophelia, Orville. . . ."

The horses' brains were swimming. The little things looked identical, and their names all blurred to one.

"I believe you were stealing those cherries," said Kit, suddenly regaining his composure. "You weren't bringing them to us. You were scooting over there toward the wood-pile to join your mate."

By now a few sheep had strayed over from the pasture to watch the exchange.

"Hold off," said May to Kit. "She gave the cherries to us. And she's right. We ought to thank her for those apples. We'd have been done with apples days ago if it hadn't been for her and those little ones."

"She's trespassing," said Kit. "I can't just let her go. She's got to leave."

"Oh, don't be so xenaphobic," called Emma from the nearby flock of sheep. "It's just a little possum. She's not hurting anything. Leave her alone."

"Yes, don't be xenaphobic," bleated the flock in chorus. "Leave her alone. Let her go back to her mate."

Let the sheep learn a new word, thought Kit, *and they'll bleat it like ninnies forever.* He was sorry the Professor had ever taught them what it meant. Now he'd never hear the end of it. Their interference had already put him off his game. He no longer felt like stomping the possum flat. He just wanted it out of his sight.

"Go on," he grumbled. "Get to the wood-pile before I change my mind."

"And don't make yourself too comfortable," he added as the possum scurried off. "Your stay here is temporary."

CHAPTER 13

By the time the corn was ripe, the animals had gotten used to having possums around. Everyone was aware that Olive and her litter were living in the wood-pile with her mate, but chose to ignore them. Autumn would be here soon, they reasoned, and the need for extra hands would vanish with the falling leaves. They could tolerate this minor infraction of their laws for the benefit of winter fruit and help with the summer harvest.

Only Gertrude was alarmed by the presence of the possums. When she saw two dragging a bucket across the yard toward the henhouse, she finally intervened.

"Just where are you going with that bucket?" she asked, blocking the entrance to the coop.

The possums stopped and eyed her curiously.

"We're taking seed to the chickens," replied the smaller one. "What does it look like?"

Gert saw that the bucket was half filled with sunflower seeds.

"That's Barlow's job," she sniffed. "You don't look like pigs to me."

The possums rolled their eyes as if they thought she were mad enough to think they were actually pigs.

"We're not pigs," they said together. "We're possums."

"I can see that," the goose snapped. "Then what are you doing here? The hens don't like strangers in their yard."

The possums stared at her with open mouths, uncertain what to make of this aggressive goose.

"What's your name?" she asked the larger possum.

"Omar."

"Does Oliver know his son is over here trespassing on the chicken yard?" she asked with narrowed eyes. "Just because Oliver's been given temporary residency doesn't mean he can invite just any-one to live here on the farm without consent."

"Oh, Oliver's not my father," said the possum. "I live in a tree by the pond."

"Not your father?" asked the goose. "Then who . . . ?"

Gertrude was stunned by the possum's impudence. With so many running about, it was impossible to keep track of who belonged and who didn't. Only the dogs could tell one from another, by smell. But as Duke complained only yesterday, with so many dif-ferent scents now intermingled throughout the farm, it was nearly impossible to identify them or keep track.

"Better watch out for Raymond," Gert said darkly, eyeing the lit-tle possums at her feet. "That rooster will cut you into bits if he sees you in there. Better leave that bucket for the pigs to deal with."

"Oh, don't worry about us," said Omar, smiling. "These seeds are for Raymond. Besides, once we've delivered them, we have to bring the eggs back to the barn so some old goose can whip them into an omelet."

The possums snickered and lifted their bucket to go.

"Some old goose . . ." stammered Gertrude as they dragged their bucket off toward the waiting rooster.

"That Raymond," she muttered. "Stupid venal bird. That popin-jay has sold himself for a scoop of sunflower seeds. I think it's time to go straighten out those pigs."

Gertrude marched over to the pigpen, still muttering to herself. Nearing the fence, she almost stopped as a rank smell of waste and rotting vegetation assailed her delicate nostrils.

"Oh dear," she said, drawing back at the sight of the pigs. Bertha and Barlow were lying on their bellies, sunk to their flanks in filth.

"What has happened to them?" she wondered. "How could they let themselves sink to such a slovenly state?"

She watched with growing alarm as a pair of young possums dragged a basket of rotten fruit toward the pigs, then dumped it in the filth and mire.

"Good work," grunted Barlow. "There," he added, tossing the possums a hunk of rotten fruit. "Here's a little something extra for your trouble."

"Did you gather the eggs?" asked Bertha, lifting her chin from the muck. "That old goose will have a fit if you don't."

The possums nodded, snickering as they dragged their empty bucket to the barn.

Those lazy pigs have stopped working, Gertrude fumed. It's just as Shep had warned. Once they quit doing chores they regressed to their filthy ways. It was time to start spreading the word about their behavior—and the growing danger of possums in their midst. With so many wild strangers running about, things were getting out of hand.

Once the harvest began, the animals were too busy to discuss the finer points of the law. Harvesting corn was a difficult affair for creatures without hands or machines. The cows and horses performed the hardest task of tearing the husks from the stalks. The dogs and pigs then carried the fallen cobs to clearings, where they piled them onto tarps so the horses and cows could drag them away for storage. The possums and raccoons, with their sharp teeth and nimble hands, proved adept at stripping some cobs for next spring's seed corn.

Gertrude tried to warn her friends and neighbors about the sudden influx of possums but was rebuffed by the impatient workers.

"Look," said Kit, staring down at her, "I'm tired. I don't have time to talk about pigs and possums. Truth is, we're all happy for the extra help. Save your worries for the next Council Meeting after the harvest. We'll talk about business then."

Gertrude herself was soon distracted by a new concern. It was her job to educate the young. The summer was quickly passing and spring chicks and foals would soon be hens and colts. Her own eggs had come late this summer, and now she had to spend the better part of each day sitting on her nest to keep them warm. Once they hatched, she'd be trailed all day by a string of goslings as she waddled about the farm conducting business. She was going to need help conducting school this year—at least till her goslings were able to look after themselves. She would have to find an assistant to help her train the next generation to perform their proper roles.

In the midst of these concerns, another crisis arose that demanded her immediate attention. Even harvesting had to stop for half a day while the animals met in a hasty Council.

"There are two sections of rail fence down," said Shep, "in the eastern stretch of the pasture. Anything could walk right through them. It's got to be dealt with immediately."

"What do you mean by 'down'?" asked Emma nervously. If there was one thing that terrified sheep, it was unwanted visitors in their pasture.

"Both rails of both sections," replied Shep. "They're on the ground. I can't tell if it's just rot or if something has chewed the rails where they fit the posts. But the two sections adjoin, leaving an awfully big gap. Those rails have got to be replaced."

"Can't use the old rails," chipped in Duke. "They're too short now and more than half rotten. Somehow we've got to make new rails and fit them back into the fence posts."

Disheartened murmurs rumbled through the Council.

"We've never cut rails before," said Raymond, who suddenly missed the steady hand of Grover, who could fashion a rail with an ax in half a minute. "What are we going to do?"

"Maybe we could find some fallen branches in the forest that fit and kind of jam them in," said Emma helpfully.

"Nope," said Shep, who'd attended many a fence repair, "we're going to have to cut them to size somehow. We'd all better put our heads together and figure out something quick. Once the wild ones spot a downed fence, they'll know there's no man here. Strong fences mean strong borders. Holes mean dead chickens and pigs."

The animals scratched their heads and fidgeted nervously, contemplating the situation. Then Rags stepped forward and made a useful suggestion.

"I know how we can get those fence rails made," he said. "I know someone who can cut them to size and fit 'em to perfection. If one or two of you will come with me, I'll go find the very fellow for the job. He lives in the woods by the river. I don't want to go there alone."

CHAPTER 14

"I'll go," said Shep, stepping forward. "Who else wants to come along?"

"I'll go," said Duke. "Jessy can stay behind and guard the fence till we get back."

With the two dogs accompanying the raccoon, additional help seemed unnecessary.

Rags smiled with satisfaction and relief.

"I would come along myself," said Pierre, stepping forward, "but someone must remain behind to protect the farm while you are gone. I will fly up to the barn's roof and serve as lookout. If danger comes, I will sound the alarm.

"Go," said the duck. "Go safe in the knowledge that the farm will be under my watch."

Shep turned to Rags, who was already eyeing the distant fence line.

"Just what kind of creature is this," Shep asked, "who can cut and fit a rail to size?"

"He's a beaver," Rags replied. "I've seen him fell a tree in less time than it takes Barlow to eat a pumpkin. He can fix that fence in a wink. But he's a stubborn fellow. He's gonna need some persuasion."

"A beaver!" cried a hen. "Not a beaver! You don't seriously mean to bring a beaver onto this farm. He's liable to kill us all!"

"A beaver is not a predator," Rags assured her. "He's quite happy eating buds and bark and twigs. And water plants, of course. He's quite a swimmer. He can stay underwater as long as a frog."

"What is he, half fish?" asked the still-reeling hen. "What sort of amphibious monster are you bringing among us? How big is this thing?"

"Almost as heavy as Duke," Rags replied. "And nearly as long when he's swimming."

"Good heavens," Duke muttered. "That big? What about his teeth?"

"Like this," said Rags, holding fingers to his mouth to show their size.

His audience gasped.

"Oh dear," muttered Shep. "Are you sure this creature's safe?"

"Safe enough," Rags replied. "If left alone. He's a bit of a hermit, living in a kind of log hut in the river. It's hard to get him to come out and talk. But one thing I know for sure," he added with a smile. "He loves corn."

Two possums delivered a burlap sack of corn to the dogs, and the three companions set off for the forest. Shep had entered the forest in the past, but always with his master and his gun. He didn't like the woods, especially the rancid moldy smells of the forest floor. He kept his nose in the air, following Rags, who having once been a resident there, knew his way about.

Shep was not afraid of what they might encounter—or even concerned about getting lost. There were few things in the forest willing to face two good-sized dogs and a big raccoon. And he and Duke could always track their scent back to the farm. What bothered him was the uncontrolled wildness of the forest; its lack of order and design. It had no borders except those imposed by the farm's stout fences, and it swarmed with animals oblivious to the law, beasts who had never known a human word or touch.

As they walked across the rugged forest floor, stepping over rotting logs and fallen branches, Shep was eager to get to the river. You could see the sky from there and catch a waft of breeze. Here in the forest, the air was dense and suffocating and far too rich with the sickening smell of rot.

At last, after a long trek over rocky ground and boulders, the trio descended a steep, moss-covered hill and spotted the muddy, slow-winding river below. Shep was impressed by Rags's inner compass. The raccoon had led them straight to a bend in the river where it pooled at a log-jam.

Looking closer, Shep realized that it wasn't a log-jam, but a dam, artfully constructed. And there in the middle of the pool was a mound of carefully arranged branches—the beaver's hut.

Shep thought, *How does the beaver get in?* There wasn't a door to be seen.

As if reading his mind, Rags said in a husky whisper, "The door's underwater. But he's probably not inside. I'll walk down to the bank and look around. Prick your ears. If he sees me, you'll know." The raccoon smiled. "And don't let him see you till I explain things a bit. If he sees two dogs, he'll panic."

Good as his word, Rags climbed over a fallen log and hiked boldly to the riverbank. As soon as he reached the water, a loud smack echoed across the pool. Then Shep heard a splash nearby.

"Hey, it's only me—Rags," called the raccoon. "Just here for a friendly visit. I brought you a gift."

Rags stood motionless for several minutes while Duke and Shep ducked behind a boulder, safely downwind.

At last, Shep spied a ripple near the water's edge. Then, like bubbling oil, the beaver's head rose out of the dark water, dripping wet.

Shep pricked his ears and listened as Rags explained their mission. At first, the beaver was rude and uninterested. Then Rags mentioned that they'd brought corn and the discussion grew more cordial.

At last Rags called out to the hidden dogs, "Hey, Duke. It's okay. Bring the sack," and the two dogs showed themselves.

Shep and Duke approached the beaver slowly, wagging their tails to show their good intentions.

The beaver eased back a little deeper into the pool as they drew near.

Rags took a fresh cornhusk from the burlap sack hanging from Duke's neck and extended it toward the beaver.

"Here," he said smiling. "Fresh off the stalk. Come on, have a bite."

"Put it there on the bank," said the beaver.

He looked uneasily at the dogs.

"So you want me to make some fence rails," he said. "Why should I? I don't trust men and farms."

"There's no man to worry about," said Rags, unintentionally giving away their secret. "The farm is run by friendly animals who would reward you with their unbounded gratitude."

"Gratitude, huh?" scoffed the beaver. "What would I do with that? What about the corn?"

"That's what I mean," said Rags. "We have acres and acres of it. A fellow like you, who'd done us such a service, would be rewarded handsomely—with more corn than you could eat."

"You don't know how much I can eat," sniffed the beaver. He eyed the cornhusk on the bank and licked his lips.

"I don't like dry land much, and I hate open spaces. I'm a river rat. Nothing can touch me here. Why should I risk my life making a fence out in the open, far from home? There are dangerous animals on a farm. Horses. Bulls. And dogs," he added with a glance toward Duke, whose panting mouth betrayed large gleaming teeth.

"We'd give you safe passage. While you worked there, you could come and go as you pleased. We could even post guards and lookouts while you worked, so you'd feel safe. If you needed a drink, we'd bring you a bucket of water. And anytime you want to eat or refresh yourself, you could rest in a safe place on the farm, in a shed or wood-pile—wherever you felt safest."

Shep almost interrupted the negotiations when Rags started talking about the beaver roaming about the farm. They were here to get a fence repaired, not take in another wild animal. But before he could complain, Rags moved the negotiations toward a settlement.

"And the best thing," the raccoon said, "is that any time you get hungry, you could slip over to the field and eat a cob or two."

"Won't take that long," said the beaver. "Four fence rails, cut and fitted. Ha! I can do it faster than it takes you to talk about it."

"Yes, but maybe later," said Rags, freewheeling now as he tried to cinch the deal. "What if in a month or two, you have a hankering for corn? Well, could we deny a meal to a fellow who fixed our fence? What are neighbors for?"

The beaver scratched his head, considering the arrangement.

"Well," he said. "A taste of corn now and again wouldn't be so bad. Hmmm. How 'bout tomorrow? Say an hour before noon, before it gets hot. I work alone. Just leave a pile of corn where you need the repair. I'll find it all right."

"And if you need someone to guard you on your way," volunteered Duke, "we'd be happy to escort you."

The beaver sniffed. "What do I look like, a chipmunk?"

He rose up and bared his front teeth. "Not much out here willing to have a go at me. Ha! I'll be there just before noon. Now hand me that sack, and the three of you get going. I like my privacy. And don't let me see you around here anytime soon."

CHAPTER 15

When the beaver arrived at the fence, he found more than a sack of corn and bucket of water waiting there. Kit and the three mares stood a short distance off, watching his every move.

After inspecting the fence and missing rails, the beaver decided how best to make the repair. In a matter of minutes he felled four saplings, stripped them of bark and limbs, and measured them to fit the fence posts. By the time he'd cut them to size, trimmed their points, and neatly installed them in the fence, the three horses had come close enough to observe his handiwork.

"That was amazing," said Kit. "Rags was right. You sure know how to work wood."

"How do you like our corn?" asked May, eager to thank the beaver for his work. "We've almost finished the harvest."

"Very good, very good indeed," said the beaver, stripping a cob and tossing it aside. He picked another from the sack and gripped it with both front paws. Then, quick as a buzz saw, he stripped the cob and swallowed a mouthful of kernels.

He sure has an appetite, thought Kit. *And those teeth! I thought I could eat, but he outstrips me.*

"Fine corn, fine corn," said the beaver, reaching for another husk. "Ummmm. Sweet. Very sweet. It sure beats river weeds."

The beaver downed another cob, then eyed the four giant horses hovering near.

"Time to go. Job's done. It's been a pleasure," he said with a glance toward the forest.

"Thank you," said May. "I sure feel safer with that fence fixed. Thanks so much for your help."

"Any time you need a repair, you know who to call. Long as you got corn," added the beaver, "I'll be available."

With that, the beaver grabbed the sack, ducked under the fence, and disappeared behind a screen of vines and leaves.

"Did you see his paws?" asked Moll after the beaver was gone.

"I'm starting to think every animal in the forest has hands," said Mara. "Maybe the so-called wild ones are farther along the path to personhood than we are."

She glanced down at her dusty black hooves. "Did you see the way he handled those saplings? Grover himself couldn't repair a fence faster than that with his ax."

"Don't be fooled," said Kit. "Did you see how eagerly he ran off to the woods? He's wild at heart, that beaver. Tameness, not hands, is what sets us apart. That beaver's well adapted to his place, but you can't turn a wild creature into a farm animal in a single lifetime. Tameness and domesticity require generations of accumulated wisdom. Kindness, gentleness, cooperation, they're what make a farm. Tameness is a spiritual achievement. Slick fur and nimble fingers don't make a wild creature tame."

Two nights later, Kit's words proved most prophetic. While strolling back to the stables, May spotted a dark shape creeping across the field. She quickly summoned the other horses and the four of them galloped across the pasture in a cloud of dust. A slow and clumsy fugitive, the thief was dragging a burlap sack and trailing stray husks of corn.

"I'll stop him," said Kit, racing to cut him off.

No match for Kit, the thief waddled away toward the woods on awkward stumbling feet. In an instant the stallion was on him. He reared up and flashed his hooves, calling out, "I've got him. Come and see."

Nosing his captive, Kit steered him toward his mates.

"It's the beaver," said Moll, staring down. She planted a hoof firmly on the sack, to pin it.

"'Course it's the beaver, who did you think it was?" snapped the surly creature at her feet. "I'm just taking home a little corn for the little ones. That's my mate over there you almost trampled to death. Is this how you treat those who come to give you help? I thought we had an arrangement."

"Your job's done," said Kit. "We paid you already. I thought you'd gone home. I didn't think you'd be coming back again."

"Yeah, sure, this job's done," replied the beaver. "But you'll be calling me again soon, I can tell you. That rail fence is old and riddled with dry rot. If you think I'll come here again to chop your saplings into rails, you've got another thing coming. Wait and see if I come to help when that fence goes down."

If one thing alarmed the horses, it was the prospect of losing their fence. It separated the pasture from the forest. Without it, they couldn't even graze in peace. They'd be watching the dark horizons from dawn to dusk.

"No need to be so defensive," said May. "We didn't say you couldn't keep the corn."

She lifted her foot off the sack. "You surprised us, that's all. We're grateful to you for repairing our fence. We won't begrudge you a little extra corn for your little ones."

"The poor things have to eat," added Moll. "We have young ones of our own. Let's stay on good terms, shall we? You never know, the time may come when you might need *our* help."

"That'll be the day," said the beaver. "Can you fell trees? Trim bark? Dam a river? Build a hutch out of logs and sticks? Can you even swim?" he asked, looking down at their heavy black hooves. "Those things look like stones."

"We can swim all right," said Kit. "And those stones drove off a pretty big bear once. Those are fine teeth you have there, beaver. But I don't think they can drive away a bear."

The beaver looked impressed but maintained a cool demeanor.

"You'd be surprised what these teeth can do. I don't reckon a bear'd like to have me open his thigh with 'em."

The beaver stared at Kit's massive hooves.

"Drove off a bear, huh?" he said with a little laugh. "Well, that's something. You're all right there, Mr. Stallion. Just leave off my mate and the two of us will get along fine.

"There," the beaver said, now addressing the mares. "How about standing back from that sack and letting us go? I'll fix your fence, all right, if you need me. Till then, you can't begrudge me the odd ear or two. It's not so easy living out there on the river. A fellow gets bored with a diet of bark and weeds."

The horses stood back and let the beavers waddle away toward the nearest fence.

Two nights later they spotted the beaver again, dragging his sack under the fence into the woods. This time they didn't pursue. It was only a few sacks of corn, they reasoned. Over the following days they got used to seeing a stray husk lying here or there about the pasture. The harvest was nearly done, and the corn would soon be safely stored away. Till then, it was worth a few ears to maintain friendly relations with their neighbor. The thought of their field being without a fence was worse than having beavers raid their corn.

Besides, with all the possums and raccoons running about, who would notice? There was no pressing need to tell their neighbors. It was the horses' field that was being crossed, and it surely needed a fence. Things were fine the way they were till winter came.

CHAPTER 16

Gertrude sat on her nest in a state of extreme agitation. There were a hundred things she had to attend to, and she was stuck here sitting on eight maturing eggs. Her mate, Gaylord, was a useless gadabout. It was up to her to warm the eggs, guard the nest, and fetch her own meals when hunger overcame her sense of duty. To top it off, her nerves were raw with anticipation. She sensed her young were about to come pecking and squeaking into the light of day, and she had business that couldn't wait. So when a helpful female possum approached and offered to sit for her, Gert quickly overcame her qualms.

"You're Olive, right? Oliver's mate? Well, I suppose you're reliable then."

"No," the possum answered with a shy smile. "I'm Olivia—but I'm very reliable. You look so tired, I thought I'd offer help."

Olive, Olivia, Gert thought, *what does it matter?* She couldn't tell one possum from another anyway. The young thing looked safe enough—and was clearly warm-blooded. All she had to do was cover some eggs for a few minutes. A warm stone could do as much.

"Okay, Olivia. All I want you to do is sit here and keep the eggs warm till I get back. Sit lightly so you don't crack them. And don't move about. Can you do that?"

She eyed the young possum closely. The little thing didn't seem very bright, but looked good-hearted and sincere.

"I'll only be gone for a few minutes. If anything happens, anything at all, have someone come and get me, okay? That's a good girl. I'll only be gone a short while."

Gert eased off the eggs and stretched her aching joints. Oh, it felt good to stand up again.

The possum gently climbed onto the eggs and curled softly about them. Gert frowned at the sight of her rat-like tail, but liked the way she carefully spread her weight over the entire nest and braced herself on its edges to keep from overburdening the eggs.

"That's good. That's just right. Don't move till I get back," Gert said, and turned from the nest and headed toward the exit.

Outside the barn, Little Rags watched as Gert went waddling off toward a grazing cow. The little raccoon was sick of cows and the very thought of milking. His hands ached from yanking fat udders and leathery teats. He was sick of barns and stools and moldy straw; of rank manure and sweaty, greasy cowhides. He'd like to burn the whole barn down and everything in it.

But most of all he was tired of picking fruit. He was tired of snipping apple stems with his teeth and picking cherries from the topmost branches for somebody else to eat. The sight of ripening pears made him almost dizzy since it meant more weeks of sore feet and aching fingers.

He wanted to go back and live in the forest again. It was fine for his parents, who were old and exhausted from years of survival in the wild. They seemed content to work from dawn till dusk to fatten the pigs. But Little Rags was a young raccoon and wanted excitement. He was old enough to remember life among tall trees and babbling streams. He was bored with eating fruit and insects. He was tired of apologizing for what he really desired.

Worst of all, his parents made him feel ashamed. He was sick of their lectures on the benefits of tameness. He didn't want to wind up like them—cringing and servile beasts fawning over their mighty lords, the cows and horses—or those nasty fearsome creatures known as dogs.

Little Rags looked up at the horseshoe nailed over the barn door and wanted to tear it down. He picked up a pebble, flung it, and hit the iron horseshoe with a clang.

Startled, the raccoon ran away toward the pond, to hide and sulk there till his troubles blew over.

"It's young Bronson," said Gert to Eudora. "He's a sturdy young pig. It's time someone gave him some chores—to keep him busy, if nothing else. It's time he pulled his weight around here. And quite a bit of weight it is, too," she added with a mirthless chuckle.

"His parents, Barlow and Bertha—they're too busy lolling about in their sty to teach him what to do. Fat lazy things. All they do is sleep and eat. How will their son learn to be a proper citizen when they act like this? Things are going to hell around here. We've got to do something quick."

"I know what you mean," replied Eudora. "It's the possums that bother me. You can't turn around without bumping into one."

Raymond, who had joined this impromptu meeting at Eudora's request, spoke up to vent his own frustrations.

"I've been meaning to tell you," he said. "We have another visitor. She's been living over in the henhouse for a while. The hens didn't tell me at first. Then I caught her nibbling seeds on the henhouse floor—a young mother quail and her six little hatchlings.

"The hens felt sorry for her, they say—because of her little ones. Now they flit all over the coop like they own the place. I think the hens envied the sheep for taking in Xena and wanted a charity case of their own.

"On top of that," he sighed, "there's a pheasant making forays into the barnyard, and I'm afraid they're going to take her under their wing as well. I overheard them whispering about it yesterday."

"Pierre has been complaining about a heron at the pond," added Eudora. "He's frightening the ducks with his long sharp bill. If one of the larger animals just made an appearance over there now and then, I'm sure he'd fly away. Poor Pierre. He looked terrible the last time I saw him. His nerves seemed pretty shot."

"Yes, but who has the time?" asked Raymond. "I'm busy enough keeping an eye on those possums—watching over the eggs and the chicks. What happened to Barlow? I thought egg-gathering was supposed to be his job."

Raymond sighed with exasperation.

"Even the dogs are confused by all the comings and goings," he said. "We never should have made that raccoon a citizen. I warned against it. But who ever listens to me?"

"We never should have let that wounded deer stay," replied Eudora. "That's where the trouble started. But it's too late now. The barn door has been opened. We've got to figure some way to close it again."

The animals nodded their heads in agreement. But before they could formulate a plan, a duck came running up with urgent news.

"It's your eggs, your eggs!" she shouted. "Your eggs are hatching!"

"My what?" shouted Gertrude. "My eggs? I told that girl to . . . Tell them I'm coming."

The goose took several running steps, spread her wings, and lifted off into the air. A few flaps took her almost to her nest, where she landed, skidding.

The sight that greeted her almost made her cry.

Olive, or Olivia, whatever the young possum's name was, was walking about the barnyard at the head of a string of goslings, which copied her every move.

The possum looked back over her shoulder, smiling as the goslings followed her in perfect file.

"You were supposed to call me," Gertrude shouted. "Why didn't you call?"

"We tried," the possum answered. "No one could find you. But it's all right, see? You have seven beautiful little ones. Lucky seven. Isn't it cute the way they follow me around?"

"Cute? Cute? You're not their mother," shouted the goose. "They're supposed to follow me. You thief. You interloper. They've been imprinted by your image."

The goose nearly cried out of fury and exasperation.

"Don't you understand?" she shouted. "Goslings follow the first thing they see! They think that you're their mother."

Her voice cracked as she sobbed, "They think you're me!"

CHAPTER 17

Gertrude tried everything she could think of to lure her goslings away from Olivia. She nestled them under her feathers, honked, flapped her wings, and displayed other goose-like behavior to arouse an appropriate response.

Sometimes, as her goslings trailed in file behind the possum, Gert brushed the imposter aside to lead them herself. But after a few steps, the little darlings always scattered in confusion till they spied the possum and chased after her again, leaving Gertrude mortified.

No matter what she did, her precious goslings refused to regard her as anything more than a kind but eccentric aunt. They called the possum "Mama Olivia," or more often "Mama." Gert—when they troubled to speak of her at all—they called "Mother."

Every time she thought about the situation, Gert had to stifle a sob.

But being freed from full-time motherhood had one unforeseen benefit. Never before had Gert felt so resolute of purpose. Though other animals were larger and more heavily armed, none were braver. She could frighten off invaders with nothing more than a honk and a daring charge. If she had to, she decided, she'd rescue the farm by herself.

Fortunately, though, Gert had two powerful allies in her friends Eudora and Shep. Though slowed by age, Eudora still commanded great respect among the animals, especially the horses and cattle. And Shep was universally regarded as the farm's most loyal and committed defender. Gert was determined to enlist both in her plan to purge the farm of trespassers. To assist in this project, she increased her surveillance of the barnyard and made secret forays into every corner of the farm, looking for something to turn to her advantage.

Finally, one day while patrolling the borders of the pond, she made a discovery that froze her in her tracks.

Little Rags the half-grown raccoon was crouched behind a tall clump of grass beside the pond, gazing through the weeds that fringed its edge. As Gertrude watched, he suddenly plunged his paws into the water and pulled out a large green frog.

After a quick glance over his shoulder to make sure no one was watching, the raccoon brought the frog closer for inspection. Then in a single motion, he snapped the poor frog's head off and swallowed it in one gulp.

After a satisfied burp, the raccoon dipped the headless torso in the pond as if to wash it, then raised it again to take a second bite.

Fighting off shock and horror, Gert reared back and let loose a honk for the ages.

Before the startled raccoon could react, she rushed him from the bushes, flapping her wings and honking like a fire engine till she'd backed him into the water, where he stood swinging the bullfrog like a Roman sword.

Before the raccoon realized that the thing storming toward him was only an old goose, Duke and Raymond roared up in a thunder of feet and wings to join the attack. Seeing that he was cornered, Little Rags dropped the frog and protested his innocence.

"I didn't do anything. I was just hungry. Leave me alone, you filthy dog. Get away from me, all of you."

By now an angry crowd surrounded the raccoon, threatening violence.

Before the situation got out of hand, Shep stepped from the crowd and seized the raccoon by the scruff of his neck. Then he dragged him away, protesting, to the distant barn.

"Get the frog," Gert commanded Duke. "That's important evidence."

Obediently, the big Lab plunged into the water and retrieved what was left of the frog. Then the crowd dispersed to follow the prisoner to his lock-up in a stall.

When word of what happened reached the ears of Little Rags's parents, they dropped their work and rushed off to the barn, bemoaning the fate of their son.

"He's broken the law," said the disconsolate raccoon to his sobbing mate. "I only hope the punishment isn't too harsh. If he did what they say, his action brings dishonor to us all. I only hope it isn't true."

The animals postponed the trial for several days till the autumn solstice, when the Council was scheduled to meet. The day was a holiday, and attendance at the meeting was expected to be large.

The incident at the pond had become a catalyst for long-simmering emotions. At Gert's insistence, the trial was scheduled to begin just prior to the Council meeting. She hoped to use it to showcase the dangers that threatened the farm.

What could better illustrate their dilemma, she thought, than a violation of a law etched into every conscience—*Do Not Kill?* Without it, tameness was impossible; a farm would be torn apart by violence. Nothing could be clearer.

As if in confirmation of her judgment, not a single animal at the trial stepped forward to defend the raccoon.

In the absence of legal counsel, Little Rags was preparing to argue his own case. Then at the last minute, he got help from an unexpected quarter. The Professor himself fluttered down from the rafters and offered to lead the defense.

Gert was almost glad to see the little barn owl involved. It was he who'd convinced them to violate their laws in the first place when he talked them into admitting that deer. Since then, it had become almost fashionable to flout the farm's laws and customs.

"It's time to pluck a few tail feathers from that pompous old bird," the goose muttered to Raymond.

"We'll have to bring him down a notch if we want to save this farm."

Gert was pleased that the rooster was prosecuting the case. He was a first-rate orator and made an impressive appearance before a jury. But behind the scenes she helped him forge an airtight case.

As the late-arriving spectators crammed the doorway to get a peek inside, the excitement was almost palpable. All eyes were on the prisoner, who stood in the dock, frowning and twisting his tail. A collection of sheep, pigs, cows, and a single horse made up the twelve members of the jury, who sat staring at the accused with hardened faces.

Then Ike the old ram entered the court, and a hush settled over the crowd.

He mounted a hay bale and peered down at the crowd with a somber expression.

"Ahem. I call this court—and this Council Meeting—to order."

He looked at Raymond.

"Mr. Prosecutor, are you ready to proceed?"

Gertrude glanced over at the rooster and gave him a silent nod.

The stage was set for the trial—and the farm's revival.

CHAPTER 18

Raymond lived up to Gert's expectations and presented a brilliant case. After calling up the witnesses one by one, he proved beyond a doubt that the raccoon had killed and eaten the frog—or at least part of him. He showed the jury the decapitated corpse and measured the size and shape of the bite, then compared it to another from the raccoon's jaws on a watermelon rind, proving the two were identical. The owl didn't challenge any of the rooster's evidence, nor object when Raymond proposed to put the defendant on the stand. Raymond called him up and interrogated him thoroughly, getting the raccoon to admit he had bitten the head off the unoffending frog. By the time the rooster ended his questioning, every animal in the room was certain that the raccoon was doomed to certain punishment.

Then the owl stepped up to the defendant and asked him a single question.

"Did you eat the frog?" he asked.

"No," said the glum raccoon. "I only bit him that one time, on the neck."

The owl turned with a smile to the jury.

"So you only bit the frog once?" he repeated. "You had no intention of eating him?"

"That's right," replied Little Rags, sensing that something had suddenly tipped in his favor. "Like I said, I only bit him that once."

Gertrude was filled with outrage. It was true that the raccoon had only bitten the frog once, but he had clearly intended to eat it. He'd washed the headless body in the pond, as if preparing his next bite, in raccoon fashion. The evil gleam in his eye clearly indicated his intentions.

She shot a quick glance toward Raymond, imploring him to make a counter move.

"The defendant *swallowed* the frog's head," the rooster interjected suddenly. "He clearly intended to eat him. And he was in the process of taking a second bite when Gertrude interrupted his assault and backed him into the pond."

The rules of order were quite informal in a trial like this. The judge let the two opponents argue back and forth to see what information emerged.

The owl turned back to the raccoon and asked in a gentle tone, "Did you bite off the head on purpose?"

"'Course not," said the raccoon, visibly brightening. "I meant to kill him, though. He's a wild creature and doesn't belong here on the farm with us domestic animals."

This statement elicited an approving murmur from the crowd. Gertrude's heart sank in her chest.

"And you didn't mean to swallow the head, did you?"

"Nope," said the raccoon. "I was surprised when it came off so easy. It nearly choked me to death."

"So you didn't want the frog on the farm?" the owl repeated, turning and smiling at the audience. "In fact, you were defending the farm, like so many other good citizens, weren't you? Just as you'd sworn to do when you took your oath and became a citizen, isn't that right?"

"That's right," said the raccoon with proudly swelling chest. "A frog ain't a farm animal. I was only doing my duty. He don't belong here."

The raccoon smiled at the audience, which responded with a smattering of applause that slowly grew in volume.

The owl let the stamping continue for a moment before he addressed the judge. Then looking up at the distinguished old ram, he said in deferential tones, "Your Honor, what exactly does the second law mean when it says 'Do Not Kill'? Does it not mean, 'Do Not Kill Other Farm Animals'?"

Ike looked nonplussed, but answered the question curtly, "That's right. It means, 'Do Not Kill Other Farm Animals.' Ahem. It's also clearly understood to mean, 'Don't Eat Them.' You can't carve all that on the wall with a couple of strokes, but that's the law's clear intent and meaning."

The owl turned with a smile toward the jury.

"We've established that Little Rags had no intention of eating the frog," he declared. "We have also reaffirmed the fact that it is sometimes necessary for a farm animal to kill a persistent trespasser to remove his threat and deter others from trespassing as well."

The owl turned to Shep and addressed the startled dog.

"Even a fine citizen like you has killed wild invaders in the line of duty, haven't you, Shep? Did you not kill and bury a groundhog only last week?"

The border collie was put off by the tone of the question but answered as well as he could.

"Yes, I had to kill him. He'd been raiding our garden all summer. I'd chased him off several times, but he only came back, sneaking underground in his tunnels to steal our food. If I didn't keep ground-hogs and rabbits out of the vegetables, they'd leave us nothing but stalks and rinds. Try living on that."

"And, Duke," the owl said, turning suddenly to address the Lab. "You killed a troublesome rat recently, didn't you? Why aren't you being prosecuted for breaking the law?

"And what about Tom and Calley?" the owl asked, turning toward the audience. "Those two brave farm cats have killed more mice between them than we can probably count . . ."

Gert tuned out the rest of the owl's clever speech, overcome by pent-up rage. The impudent little bird had turned the whole thing around. It was infuriating the way he made it look like murdering and eating an innocent frog was the same as driving off hungry predators or killing rapacious vermin. She could already foresee the trial's inevitable conclusion.

But the owl's closing argument took a startling new turn.

"Gert," called the Professor, shocking her out of her reverie. "Wasn't the only reason you assaulted this innocent raccoon and accused him of a crime the fact that he is a newcomer? Wasn't his crime only that he once lived in the forest? Had you forgotten that he is a citizen, like you?"

The owl shook his head sadly.

"Weren't your actions impelled by nothing more than xenophobia?"

The trial ended as Gert expected, with the raccoon's acquittal. Worse, it ended with a chorus of sheep bleating *"Xenaphobia!"* in her ears.

When the raccoon received his verdict, the barn erupted in applause. Pigs filed past to clap Little Rags on the back, and the horses broke into hearty congratulations. The raccoon's vicious murder had made him a hero.

The only animal convicted of wrongdoing, Gert thought ruefully, was her. She felt the hot eyes of pigs and sheep burning the back of her head like glowing embers. She turned away, blinded by tears.

Then she thought of the Council Meeting with a smile. The real showdown still lay ahead. These uninvited guests, these unlawful trespassers, would face justice at last. The farm would still return to what it had been before they came.

CHAPTER 19

In her opening remarks before the Council, Eudora urged the animals of Green Pastures Farm to remember how clear and simple their lives used to be before the wild animals arrived. Now the newcomers seemed to be everywhere; lurking in the shadows and intruding on every aspect of their lives. The presence of so many strangers, Eudora argued, endangered the farm's security, which depended on a strict adherence to the law. The woods were full of enemies waiting to take advantage of any weakness. With so many aliens running about the farm, it was no longer possible to tell friend from foe. The dogs were worn out trying to separate those who belonged from those who didn't. Policing the borders was becoming impossible. The time had come to round up all the non-citizens and expel them for the good of all.

"It's not just the threat to our lives," the old cow admonished them. "It's what it's doing to our way of life. The farm is changing, and not for the better. I'm not the only one who's noticed what's been happening around here. There are others who have asked to speak this afternoon about what needs to be done to preserve our way of life."

Eudora signaled a pair of hens to step forward and tell their stories. The first spoke in a voice pinched tight by fear.

"The chickens don't like having possums working in our coop," she said with a nervous glance toward Oliver, who was sitting nearby. "They make us nervous. It was bad enough when there was just one or two and they worked under close supervision, but now they're everywhere. When I was a wee little chick, my grandmother told me stories about midnight raids by creatures who looked an awful lot like our new residents. There's no telling what they might do when left alone. They're wild after all, aren't they? Not civilized creatures, like hens, and dogs, and cows. You cattle and horses might find our fear amusing, but try living every day among wild creatures twice your size, with toothy smiles that remind you why fences were built in the first place."

Her piece said, the first hen stepped back and gave the floor to her friend.

"I caught a young possum trying to steal one of my eggs," she said with trembling voice. "Those shifty little creatures shouldn't be left unsupervised to gather our night's production. I just wonder how many other eggs have been stolen since those possums took the job. More than a few, I reckon. I thought the pigs were supposed to be performing that particular serv—"

"Wait a minute," interjected Barlow, stepping forward to state his case. "That possum wasn't stealing your egg. She was taking one that had been overlooked to Opal, who was gathering them for the morning bucket. The egg was left behind by mistake. That's all there is to that story. Don't get so worked up over trifles."

"She was walking the wrong way," scoffed the hen. "She wasn't taking it to any bucket. And don't tell me not to get worked up. Why weren't you there doing your job, the way you're supposed to?" she demanded. "Instead of lying around that filthy sty of yours from morning till night, ordering possums about?"

"Speaking of eggs," piped in Gertrude before Barlow could respond to the hen's attack, "one of my own precious eggs was stolen from my nest not long ago—I won't say by whom. I counted eight before I let that young Olivia sit on them for me. By the time I got back—from a very important engagement, or I wouldn't have left— there were only seven goslings hatched. A mother goose knows how many young she's got. In such matters, we don't make mistakes. And

I haven't even mentioned the pain I feel every time I see my little ones following around that little marsupial miss like she's their mother."

Loud honks of agreement rose from her fellow geese.

Then a voice from the back of the barn spoke up from a delegation of Hereford cows.

"There are beavers sneaking onto the farm at night. They're stealing corn right out from under our noses. The horses know about it, but they're doing nothing to stop the practice. There are kernels strewn all across the pastures from beavers eating on the run. The main culprit's that one who patched our broken fence, but there's more than him involved. They're taking it to their friends out in the wild—whole sacks of fresh-picked corn. If we let that go on, there'll soon be none for us when the cold weather comes."

"There's only so much grass in the fields," chimed in a ewe, over the protest of her neighbors. "Those who let a certain injured doe and her two fawns sleep in our shed better think about that. It's fine to be generous and kind, that's one thing; but at some point you've got to draw the line and say NO MORE."

A few sheep bleated support, but the rest quickly drowned them out with cries of "xenaphobia." Eudora had to call them to order so that Pierre could have his say.

"It's their incessant nocturnal activity that we can't abide," the duck began. "My senses, as everyone knows, are attuned to the slightest danger. I am known throughout the farm as an incomparable sentinel. Yet I find it nearly impossible to keep an effective watch when little feet are scurrying about the farm all night, picking fruit or making a general nuisance of themselves. I can hardly sleep through their infernal activity—which is in clear violation of our law.

"'Walk by Day, Not by Night.' There's nothing ambiguous about that. Yet some find it impossible to live by such a code. I tell you, the time has come to return to strict enforcement of our laws. To do less is to court disaster."

"Wait a minute," cried out Bertha. "You all forget what life was like here before Rags and the others came to help us pick the fruit. Most of our crop just rotted on the stem. Look at us now," she said. "We've never had so much fruit—or beans, or corn. We've never enjoyed such prosperity. They're not here to change the way we live. They're only looking for a better life for themselves. They're mostly doing jobs that none us can even do."

"You mean *want* to do," shot back an angry hen.

"All right, then, don't *want* to do," interjected Barlow in defense of his mate.

"If you insist on perfect honesty, there are some jobs I'd rather not do, I don't mind saying. I don't see any great disadvantage in letting those equipped with little hands gather the eggs from the chicken coop. It hurts my mouth dragging that bucket across the yard. Try hauling your own eggs for once and you'll see what I mean."

The pig's remark was answered by an indignant clamor from the chickens. Eudora had to stamp her foot and call for order several times before anything could be heard over their squawks.

"The point is," the old cow declared, "we used to do these jobs ourselves. Maybe we didn't pick every apple or pear, but we never starved. Hard work builds character, it gives us pride in who we are. In performing our daily tasks, we learn to trust and depend upon each other—because our own success depends on our service to the farm. Turning our jobs over to others might seem like a bargain at first, but it makes us weak. When the day comes to defend the farm again, our jaws and limbs might lack the strength—and our spines the necessary iron—to make a stand."

All across the barn heads nodded in quiet agreement. Eudora's words roused the patriotism of her fellow citizens and made some blush for shame. If at that moment the old cow had proposed to expel all of the trespassers, the vote would have been nearly unanimous in her favor. But then Rags, the old raccoon, stepped forward and humbly begged to speak.

CHAPTER 20

"First, I want to thank you all for letting me and the missus and Little Rags live here among you on this beautiful farm," the raccoon began. "We are proud to be members of this community. We hope someday to be as tame and domesticated as you. Your laws and traditions have given us the first peace and security of our lives."

Rags cast a grateful smile toward the assembly, which seemed touched by his heartfelt words.

"Though we have never known the touch or words of man," the raccoon continued in a husky voice, "we hope to learn to walk in his ways, like you. As you've shown today in your treatment of my son, your laws are just and fair—and apply to all, without regard to size or rank or species. I don't say I'm worthy of being a citizen, but I am honored that you've given me that title. I only hope that when you talk of expelling trespassers, you don't mean to include us humble raccoons. We're small and gentle folk—though forest-born—and so perhaps not worthy of the privileges you've conferred on us. But please, when you decide what to do, give a thought to old Rags—a proud citizen who would give his life to save Green Pastures Farm— or the life of anyone on it."

With that, the raccoon bowed modestly and shuffled back into the crowd to join his family.

The mood in the barn changed. When Shep stepped forward to speak, he sensed a new self-consciousness among his friends and neighbors. It was one thing to talk about defending the farm against wild animals when they lived on the other side of the fence. But now, with raccoons and possums listening in, it was hard to speak candidly. The eyes of Rags and Oliver were only the most visible of their observers. Others listened from the shadows and beneath the floorboards. It took a surprising degree of determination to stand up and speak his mind.

"It's not that we can't find and identify the wild ones," Shep began. "There are possums in wood-piles and hay bales all over the farm. Right now there are several possums living under the floor of the henhouse, not to mention all those tucked away in the sty. If we could agree to expel them all, we dogs could find and root them out one by one. But we need cooperation from our neighbors. I can't corner a possum and then be told by an angry pig not to chase him because he's a worker in the orchard. Far as I know, he's a thief. Or just when I'm about to make some strange raccoon answer for trespassing, have a ewe jump in and say I shouldn't touch him because he's carrying buckets or doing some other chore—and then look at me like I'm the one breaking the law."

Shep looked imploringly at the horses and cattle near the door.

"You probably don't know about this," he said, "but a while back the sheep had a secret vote making it illegal to cooperate with us when we're hunting for trespassers in their pasture. The other day I caught a young buck in the sheep shed, and when I asked what he was doing there, Emma jumped in and told me it was illegal to inquire about the status of their residents.

"'What have you got against hoofed creatures?' she asked, as if I was in the wrong. She told me to mind my own business and shooed me back toward the barn

"How can I do my job with that kind of attitude?" Shep asked plaintively. "Just give the word, and Duke, Jessy, and I will root out trespassers. If we each do our part, we can have the farm back the way it was—with no stolen eggs and no little ones living in fear for their lives. If we don't make a stand now, someday we'll be outnumbered. We've got to get the wild ones out while we still can."

"That's ridiculous," snorted Barlow. "Outnumbered. Living in fear for their lives."

The pig chuckled. "I can just see the pasture overrun by a herd of rampaging possums. Poor Kit and the mares—helpless against all those tiny grasping hands."

The assembly laughed at Barlow's joke—none louder than Kit, who joined in the general levity.

"I'd better warn Garth to be on his guard," quipped the stallion. "Once they overrun our pasture, they're coming for the cattle. Looks like that great hulking bull's finally going to meet his match."

The crowd laughed again—till Gert took a jab of her own. "Is that you talking, Kit—or just a taste for apples?"

The goose glared at the horse, then stared down the mocking crowd.

"I don't think this is an occasion for humor," she said. "When did the mighty Kit—hero of our stand against the bear—become a champion for trespassers? Sometimes I wonder if this is the same farm I'm living on as on that sacred day."

"Come on, Gert," the stallion pleaded. "I was only joking. But you have to admit, the possums and raccoons don't pose much of a threat. Besides, it's impractical at this stage to round them up and chase them off. There are too many, and we need their help on the farm. The benefits of letting them stay outweigh the risks. I say we find some way to work things out."

"If having illegal possums is a problem," piped up Mara, "why don't we just make them legal, the way we did Rags. Then the problem's gone. We could offer a pardon to any wild creature who wants to become a citizen. They'd feel more welcomed by us, and we could stop worrying about having so many non-citizens about, causing confusion."

"Why don't we declare the rain dry and then we won't get soaked in a storm?" cried an angry chicken. "What's the point of having fences if we let wild creatures in?"

The discussion stalled as the two sides squabbled back and forth, throwing verbal jabs and insults. Then, as the hubbub diminished, a voice spoke from above.

"At the risk of seeming pedantic," it said in soothing tones, "let me address that chicken's excellent question."

As all eyes turned toward the rafters, the Professor floated down to settle on an unoccupied hay bale.

"You all speak as if having so many diverse creatures on the farm is a disadvantage," he said with a smile. "When in fact, it is a great social benefit, reflecting one of nature's greatest principles: *Biodiversity.*"

"Biodiversity?" called out a chicken, scratching her head. "What on earth is that?"

"Biodiversity, my friends," replied the owl, "is the idea that the more various forms of life there are in a given environment, the better the chances are that all will thrive and be happily interdependent. This holds true not only for the forest, but for the farm as well.

"Take those eggs, for instance," he said, "the subject here tonight of so much debate. If chickens were banned from the farm, like beavers and possums, then we wouldn't have eggs for the dogs and pigs to eat. The chickens provide the dogs with food, and the dogs in turn provide the chickens with security. That, my friends, is biodiversity in a nutshell."

The Professor smiled.

"For another example of this great principle in action, consider our recent additions to the farm: Rags and his fine family of raccoons. Once they were considered trespassers and driven off. The result? No one to pick fruit from the treetops. Enter the raccoons, and what results? A bountiful harvest for all.

"That's biodiversity," concluded the owl. "If you looked at your laws, you would see that very principle embodied in your own constitution: '*Many Animals, One Farm.*'"

The owl blinked his liquid eyes at the assembly.

"Looked at properly, biodiversity is an extension of your own best ideals—to spread tameness and domesticity throughout the world. Is that not so? What could better ensure your ultimate security than increasing the ratio of tameness to wildness in the world?

"Think of it," the owl said with a pointed look at Gertrude. "By taking the forest creatures in and converting them, you would be forwarding your own noble cause of spreading domesticity. In time, by taming the lawless creatures of the forest, you will have no ene-mies left to threaten your lives."

Nods of agreement bobbed across the room. Calls of "That's right!" rang out above the general murmur.

"If you will be kind enough to allow me one last suggestion," the owl continued, "I think I can offer a practical solution to your prob-lem—that is, how to deal with what you mistakenly call 'trespassers' on the farm. The answer in a word, my friends, is *education*. If Green Pastures Farm is to be more than just an isolated refuge in a sea of hostility forever under siege, it must become the educator of the world."

The owl paused to let his listeners consider the idea.

"Where else will such wise and clever creatures be found as right here on this farm?" he asked with a smile. "With teachers such as Gertrude and Eudora to instruct them, the most ignorant beasts, the most untamed savages, will surrender their wildness and become productive citizens."

The owl turned, beaming sweetness, to the ram.

"Under the religious instruction of Ike," he continued with mounting enthusiasm, "the bear might learn to plow, the lion to guard his fellow citizen the lamb. The humble goose might instruct the eagle how to take his meals, and the dog teach the wolf how to lead and tend the herd. In short, if you practice the noble principle of Biodiversity, you will become more prosperous, happy, and secure. You will look back upon the days when you excluded the forest creatures from your community as an age of unenlightened darkness and superstition.

"As our brave friend Kit has already suggested, you can begin the next phase of your bold experiment in self-government by offering a general amnesty to all those drawn to this beacon of hope and rea-son. Then you must start a school, to educate your new residents in tameness, so the farm can reap the benefit of greater biodiversity.

"Gertrude," the owl called to the startled goose, "you must become the Superintendent of this new enterprise. I can already foresee many possible fields of study. Perhaps the beaver who fixed your fence could offer a course in maintenance and repair. Shep might teach a course in tracking and herding. The horses might teach the slow-footed how to run, and the sheep instruct the uncultured in manners and etiquette."

Barlow and Bertha grunted approval, nodding at the owl's sagacity.

"And if you will allow me," added the Professor with a final bow, "I would like to offer you the benefit of my own wide learning and experience and assist you in developing your school's curriculum. Later, perhaps I can conduct the odd seminar or two for advanced students."

By the time the Professor finished, the audience was stamping and braying approval. The vote to grant a general amnesty was nearly unanimous. Gertrude was so caught up in the idea of supervising the new school that she almost cried out in support herself.

She didn't dare look at Shep, who seemed crushed by this unexpected turn. The poor fellow was a dogged advocate. Once put on a scent, it wasn't easy to call him off.

She'd reconcile with him later, she decided, after the meeting, and convince him of the wisdom of the plan. In the meantime, there were a million things to think about.

First, she'd get together with the owl in the morning and select instructors. Then they'd discuss the general curriculum. Together, they'd lay the intellectual foundation for Green Pastures College, abolish the five houses' makeshift schools, and educate all the young animals together in a proper Preparatory School.

CHAPTER 21

Though initially shocked by the sheer number of wild animals living on the farm, Gertrude soon saw them as potential students. She quickly established a fast-track course on citizenship, and after an intensive two-day training period, the new residents graduated and took their oath en masse.

The possums already living in the pigpen were assigned to live with Bertha and Barlow. Others were scattered among the stables, henhouse, and orchards. The mother quail and her young were absorbed by the chicken coop and the sheep admitted the young buck and doe along with their ailing mother.

Only one of the several beavers that had been raiding the farm decided to stay and become a citizen. The half-grown orphan named "Tooth" lived in the barn and was assigned with Shep and Jessy to fence patrol, where his job was to make on-site repairs to damaged rails.

Once the new citizens were happily settled in their new jobs and homes, they signed up for classes in the new school along with their farm-born neighbors.

The academic term began with the onset of autumn. On the first cold morning of October, the school day opened with a recital of the farm's four laws by the entire student body. Then after a class in picking fruit conducted by Oliver, the farm's first possum, the students filed into the dark confines of the barn for Chapel, where Ike preached a sermon on tameness and students led prayers to the spirit-shepherd. Then the students all marched out to the barnyard for recess and an hour of rough-and-tumble play.

In the afternoon, the Professor taught a seminar in constitutional law to the half-grown young and yearlings who had already been trained at home in basic skills by their parents.

For this first year, Gertrude told the barn owl to focus on basic principles, beginning with *Many Animals, One Farm*, to help the students adapt to their new life. Most of her own time was now spent in her office, overseeing the curriculum and counseling students at a makeshift hay bale desk in the barn.

Above her desk hung a sign, whose crudely scratched symbols proclaimed the school's motto:

STRENGTH THROUGH BIODIVERSITY.

Personally, Gertrude would have preferred one that said WALK BY DAY, NOT BY NIGHT, to remind students to observe the unfamiliar custom—but the owl's slogan had already taken hold.

On afternoons when Gertrude finished work early, she sometimes visited classes. Today, perhaps reminded by the sign, she decided to visit his seminar to see how the students were learning.

To keep her presence from distracting the class, she crept up to the edge of the barnyard and watched from behind a broken wagon wheel.

The little Professor was pacing up and down a fence rail, leading the class in a discussion of the first law.

Everyone seemed to be listening attentively. Even the chickens had left off scratching the ground to hear what the wise Professor said.

"As we have seen in our earlier discussions," the Professor continued, pacing back and forth on the wooden rail, "the law 'Many Animals, One Farm' leads inevitably to the doctrine we call 'Many-Animalism.'

"Until recently, this doctrine was not fully applied here on Green Pastures Farm.

"While it is true," he quickly added, "that the farm's laws did enforce a rough equality between large and small, swift and slow, powerful and weak, there remained various forms of inequality.

"Why is it, for instance," he asked, suddenly looking down at a startled ewe, "that the dogs feel free to chase the sheep from field to barn whenever they feel the urge?"

He scanned the sea of heads, waiting for an answer.

Finally, little Pip called out from the rear, "Because sometimes the sheep won't come into the barn on time, even if there's danger or bad weather."

The owl's face assumed a wry, sardonic look as he strolled slowly down the rail.

"That comment is a perfect example of what I'm talking about," he said. "Being a dog yourself, you are limited by your own canine perspective. You can't see the validity of the sheep's position, which is in every way the equal of your own.

"In fact, your answer presumes your superiority—to an animal with its own nature, habits, and customs—merely because it is different from you. Perhaps sheep move to a slower rhythm than a hyperventilating dog."

The class laughed at the pup's embarrassed reaction.

"Have you ever considered," asked the owl, "that your urge to herd arises from a desire to dominate?"

The owl winked down at a ewe.

"The notion that all animals are alike and interchangeable, embodied in the second half of the law, 'One Farm' is founded on violence and a presumed right to dominate. Many-Animalism corrects that mistaken emphasis—that discriminatory bias, as it were—by returning to the truth embodied in the first half of the law: '*Many Animals.*'

"Remember, forcing all animals to fit one mold is a form of breedism. And breedism is always informed and upheld by violence.

"You," the owl said, pointing back toward Pip. "How does a dog get the sheep to move in the same direction if they start to stray?"

"Well," answered Pip unsurely, "he might run at them and pull up at the last second to kind of steer them in the right direction."

"Meaning," replied the owl, "that he pretends he's going to crash bodily into the poor sheep and so he startles them into motion out of fear."

The owl smiled.

"But what if the sheep decide not to move at all?" he asked. "Even if he runs directly at them? What if they don't fall for his feint?"

"I guess it depends on the situation," the dog replied. "If a coyote, say, has been spotted near the pasture, and the dog wants to steer them away from there as fast as he can, he might have to sort of run up and nip one on the heel to sort of get them going in the right direction."

Pip saw the trap he'd fallen into even before the Professor spoke.

"He's not really trying to hurt the sheep," Pip stammered in his defense. "Sheep can be awful frustrating sometimes when they refuse to . . ."

Defeated, Pip abandoned his argument as the other students frowned and shook their heads.

Satisfied, the Professor paced back down the rail, resuming his lecture.

"Let's turn now to the second law: 'Hoof, Web, Paw, Claw—On Level Ground, Under One Law,' to use Gertrude's charming version.

"Too often we concentrate our attention on the 'level ground' provision, ignoring the *difference* it elides between hoof and web, paw and claw. By contrast, Many-Animalism teaches us to appreciate difference. It teaches us to appreciate and respect our own identity— as well as the identity of others."

The owl paused from his lecture to take questions from the students.

"But we can all vote just the same, can't we?" called out a possum. "I mean, now that we're citizens and all."

"Yes, vote," replied the owl sardonically. "But how many possums hold office here on the farm?"

The class grew still and silent.

"Yes, exactly," chuckled the Professor—and pointed toward the distant fence.

"And what about all the possums in the forest?" he asked, suddenly. "Can they vote here?"

"'Course not," called out Bronson. "They ain't citizens like us."

"You mean," replied the owl, "because someone drew an arbitrary line called a fence, some possums have no rights to a decent existence like you and your kin? It's all right if they go hungry this winter—and perhaps even starve? Whereas, if they merely step across that line and say a few words, they deserve the same food and shelter—and right to vote—as you?"

For a moment the class fell silent again, turning blankly to one another.

Then Pip called out, "But they're *wild*. They don't live here. They're not tame and domesticated like us."

The Professor peered down at the student in front of him.

"Look at Ophelia sitting here in front of me. She's a possum. Are you saying she can't live here because she's wild?"

"That's breedism," shouted Oscar, rising to defend his cousin. "Professor, that dog is a flat-out breedist. That dog's got no business here."

Rather than intervene, the Professor continued to pace up and down the fence.

A few ducks and hens muttered quietly, "Well, they are possums, aren't they? They oughta be thankful they're living here."

"So you think dogs and pigs deserve to live in safety and comfort," continued the owl, "and enjoy the freedom to vote, but possums, and raccoons, and beavers deserve to live in fear and starve? Is that what you're saying?" he asked, ignoring the hens as he directed his question at Pip.

"Why don't they start their own farm instead of coming here if they're so tame?" muttered Bronson loudly enough to be heard. He was a hefty young pig and had no fear of possums.

"Why don't you go back to the woods if you don't like it here?" he said a bit louder so the possums and raccoons could hear. "I'll pick my own apples, if it comes to that."

"Fat pig couldn't pick his own nose," countered Little Rags, provoking laughter from his friends.

To stop the descent into insults, the Professor turned back to Pip with a quizzical expression.

"You said the possums were kept on the other side of the fence because they're wild. But what does that mean to be *wild*? And what does it mean to be *tame*? That sort of binary thinking is a product of breedism. Yes, breedism. Arbitrarily splitting animals into opposite categories involves a kind of violence."

The owl pointed toward the distant pasture.

"Are the salamanders living under the rocks in the stream domesticated farm animals or wild creatures of the forest?" he asked. "They live on the farm; therefore, they would appear to be farm animals. They don't harm their fellow citizens; therefore, they're tame. Why don't they hold citizenship and vote? Why do you feel so superior to them, my fine young citizen—is it merely because you're larger and more powerful?

"What about the birds that perch in the orchards? What are they? Citizens or trespassers? They don't feed on hens or sheep, do they, when no one's looking? I'd say they were at least as tame as pigs, who have been known on occasion to do violence to hens—or to others—by means of careless words."

The owl turned back and glared at the young pig.

"What about foxes?" answered Pip, growing defensive on behalf of his best friend. "Are we supposed to let them on the farm, too?"

"Funny you should mention foxes," the owl said, smiling. "Of all creatures. Why, they're canines, just like you. Same big sharp teeth. Same cunning and ferocity. Do you feel more closely related to a fine young fox—or a tiny defenseless chick?"

The other students looked at the dog nervously, to see how he'd respond. It had never occurred to them to think of dogs that way. Now that they did, they could see the resemblance. Looked at with opened eyes, dogs were rather terrifying.

As for Gertrude, behind her wagon wheel she was left gasping by the owl's discussion. She had to stop listening and tiptoe back into the shadows to catch her breath and clear her mind. The owl's lecture wasn't anything like she'd envisioned. In fact, it was unsettling and dangerous—not at all what they'd agreed on. She would speak to the owl in the morning before class.

If the school was going to turn youngsters into productive, law-abiding citizens, she'd have to keep a tighter rein on things.

CHAPTER 22

Despite Gertrude's misgivings about the owl, her school seemed to be teaching the new citizens about their laws. Soon after learning about their constitutional rights, the possums living in the pigpen decided to put their lessons to work by calling a meeting to discuss the assignment of chores. When all the pen's residents were in attendance, Olive called them to order by hammering the floor with a tenpenny nail.

"The law says every animal has one ear and one voice," she said with a significant glance at the pigs. "I just want to make sure we all agree on its meaning."

"We understand it, all right," sighed Bertha. "So could you tell us what this meeting's about? I'm getting hungry. I could use a bucket of apples—or maybe dried pears—to take the edge off my appetite till the evening bucket arrives."

"That's just what I'm getting to," replied Olive. "I think it's time we took a vote on who has to fetch the food."

"What's there to vote on?" asked Barlow impatiently. "That's Omar's job—or is it Oscar? I never was sure."

"Why me?" demanded the possum in question, Oscar. "I never asked to do it. I don't even like apples, so why would I want to carry a bucket halfway across the farm? Only reason I got stuck doing it is 'cause you said I had to, back before I was a citizen. I don't remember putting it to a vote."

"That's what we're here for today," declared Olive, resuming control. "Would someone please make a motion so we can put the issue to a vote?"

"Put what to a vote?" demanded Barlow with a laugh. "I'm not about to start hauling buckets around here again. Been there, done that. It's time for a change."

"So you think you can still say who does what around here?" shot back Oscar. "Look around you, pig. You're outnumbered. I'll make the motion, then, if no one else will," he said with a snort.

"I move that a pig bring the meal bucket over here when it's time to eat."

"I second the motion," said Omar. "I'm sick of doing all the work around here."

"Wait a minute," said Barlow more reasonably. "You don't mean to say you're really going to ask us to bring you your meals, do you? After all, we were kind enough to let you live here with us in our pen. We took you in and gave you a place to live before you were even citizens. Heck, I argued to grant you all pardons so you could enjoy full citizenship and share in our farm's prosperity. You can't turn around and tell me I have to serve you breakfast now. It wouldn't be right."

"All who want to have a pig bring the meal buckets to the pen vote by saying 'Aye,'" said the chair.

"Aye," said the possums in unison.

"Those opposed, say 'Nay.'"

"Nay," shouted Bertha, while Barlow almost choked sputtering, "Wait a minute, this can't be happening. . . . You don't really mean to . . ."

"Motion passes," said Olive. "A pig will now carry all meal buckets from the barn to the sty."

"What about the morning egg bucket?" asked Opal. "And taking feed to the chickens?"

"You have to make a motion," replied the chair.

"I move that a pig be responsible for feeding the chickens and taking their eggs to the barn," Opal said, correcting herself. "Every morning of the week."

"All in favor?"

The motion passed again. Bertha provided the only nay vote while her mate continued to plead with the possums to reconsider their plan.

"All right," he finally conceded. "If you're hell-bent on living off our sweat, at least let our boy Bronson take over the job. He's a strong young pig—though a bit spoiled—and could use a little exercise."

"You have to make that a motion," said the chair.

"All right, all right, I move that Bronson take over all jobs involving bucket carrying," said Barlow in exasperation. He sat down with a heavy sigh.

"All in favor?"

"Aye."

"The motion passes," said Olive. "It's settled then. Bronson will carry the buckets."

The others nodded with satisfaction and began to drift toward the door.

"Thank heaven," sighed Barlow. "The thought of dragging that bucket every morning again makes my teeth hurt. You'll tell Bronson how the vote went, won't you, dear?" he asked his bewildered mate. "He's a willful boy and doesn't always listen to me. Try to explain it in a way he'll understand."

A similar scene was enacted the next day in the henhouse. Dusk was nearing as the resident mother quail looked up at the roost and asked, "Why is it that the rooster always gets to sit at the top, by the door? Who elected him king?"

The chickens clucked among themselves for a moment, considering the quail's question. Then Hetty stepped forward to explain.

"It's because he's the rooster. He needs to sit up high so he can keep an eye on things."

"But why can't he keep an eye on things from down here where I sleep, on the floor? I sure wouldn't mind having a nice roost to sit on way up there, where I can breathe a little fresh air and almost feel the sky."

"You don't understand," replied Hetty. "Raymond has to watch over the coop and the chicken yard. Someone has to keep an eye on things, or we wouldn't be safe."

A large raccoon, known simply as "Miss Gray," scoffed openly at Hetty's assertion.

"Keep watch, hmmmph. I'd like to know how he keeps watch with his eyes closed all night. Why don't you let someone keep watch who has a feel for the night, like me? I don't mind saying I have trouble sleeping in the dark. Seems like the time to be up and doing. But I sit in here every night, watching and listening as I drift in and out of sleep. I could keep a better watch than that sleepy bird anytime. And it'd give me something to do to pass the time."

"No, no, no, you don't understand," insisted Hetty. "A chicken coop is a dangerous place. There are thieves and marauders lurking about, waiting to take advantage. Raymond is a fearsome warrior when he's aroused. One summer he killed a big black snake. There's more to keeping watch than just keeping an eye out. You have to have the courage to face trouble when it comes along—and the sharp beak and spurs to tear a trespasser apart."

"Tear a trespasser apart," sniffed the raccoon. "Large black snake—it was probably only a little garter snake. Why, I've killed snakes that could swallow that rooster whole—and eaten them down like noodles. And as far as beaks and spurs are concerned, take a look at these."

The raccoon retracted her lips, revealing a muzzle full of gleaming pointy teeth.

The chickens sucked in their breath and took a quick step back.

"Why don't we put it to a vote then?" asked the quail. "Why shouldn't someone else have the privilege of sitting up there now and then?"

Hetty continued clucking about the necessity of keeping Raymond happy and confident in his role of protector, but the other hens had already been won over by the raccoon's logic.

"All right then, I say let's vote on who gets to sit on top," cried an excited little hen. "I'm for Miss Gray here. Looks to me like she's got the right equipment for the job."

"I move that Miss Gray get top rung," chipped in the quail. "It's time somebody brought that pompous rooster down a notch. It's not like we need him looking after us now, with the dogs and raccoons and possums living so close by.

"All in favor," said the quail, "say 'Aye.'"

"Aye," shouted the henhouse with one voice.

"While we're on the subject," called out the little hen, "why don't we vote on the second roost, too? Why should little Miss Hetty get to sit up there every night beside her lord and master? I say the second rung should rotate between us all on a nightly basis."

A motion to rotate the second rung was made and quickly passed. The chicken coop was filled with the excitement of novelty. The hens clucked with an undercurrent of glee at the prospect of discomfiting the rooster, who'd been lording it over them all for a long time now. Understandably, Hetty was downcast at the prospect of losing her roost beside the dashing and handsome rooster and angry at the pettiness of the others, who, it seemed to her, were being shortsighted. Raymond had risked his life more than once to protect them and their eggs and little chicks. She wasn't sure that toothy Miss Gray would serve as well.

From the looks of those choppers, she thought privately, it might even be a good idea to keep a watch on her.

CHAPTER 23

"It's an outrage," said Raymond. "They've taken away my roost. I've been replaced by a female raccoon of dubious reputation, and the whole henhouse is delirious with glee."

"I know what you mean," sighed Barlow. "My son Bronson is now hauling food buckets for the possums.

"You were right," he said, turning to Shep. "It was a mistake letting so many wild animals on the farm. Now there's no getting rid of them."

"It's no use chasing them down anymore," Shep agreed. "Soon as I chase one off, he's back again within hours. If there weren't a single wild possum or raccoon on the farm, then we'd know what to do when we saw one. As it is, we can't keep them out. The ones that are here hide their cousins and friends—or take them food in the woods till they can sneak in. It's like trying to stop the stream from overflowing its banks."

Shep scraped his paw through the dust of a raccoon's paw print.

"I caught a ferret yesterday near the chicken coop," he said quietly. "He ducked into a hole before I could catch him and came up a few feet away inside a tree stump, where I couldn't dig him out. I called down and warned him to stay off the farm. I said the next time I saw him would be his last—and you know what he said?"

Shep looked up at Eudora with a furrowed brow.

"He said he'd been invited by the chickens to help with pest control. Said there were mice under the floor boards, and he'd been called in from the forest to do a job that we can't."

"He's just telling tales," replied Eudora, "because you had him cornered. The hens aren't fools enough to invite a ferret into their house."

"Ha!" exclaimed Raymond. "Try talking to Hetty about that. She says they've lost all sense and reason. They're drunk on changing everything to suit their new hero, that blasted Miss Gray.

"Before you know it," the rooster exclaimed, "she'll be trying to crow the sun up. Let's see her read the stars. Let's see her tell when it's planting time—or harvest. Thinks she can do my job, does she? Why, if she weren't so big and didn't have that set of monstrous teeth. . . ."

"There's no use moping," said Gertrude, recalling how her eager young students were learning to appreciate the farm's way of life. "Things might not be exactly the way we'd like, but they are starting to settle down. It's the novelty, that's all—it'll soon wear off. All the excitement of the new school, so much learning going on across the farm—it's downright inspiring.

"Anyway," she added hopefully, "it's almost time for the fall pageant. The play will teach the newcomers about our heroic traditions, like defeating the bear and learning to run the farm. You'll see. I'm so busy with the new teachers this year that I've appointed Olivia to run the show.

"I do love theatricals, though," she muttered to herself, "so perhaps next season. . . .

"I've taught her last year's script, which was such a big hit, so I don't see how it could fail."

Gert looked into the distance as her voice trailed off.

"Anyway, I'm sure Olivia can direct the play. She ought to be good at play acting," she muttered. "She's been pretending to be a goose since the day my goslings hatched."

The next day, while patrolling the fence line with young Pip, Shep tried to explain the importance of maintaining borders. It was up to the dogs to lead the way in such matters, he said. Pip was almost full-grown and someday when this business of trespassers was back under control, he'd have to do the job himself.

"But why do we have to keep out the beavers and ferrets?" asked Pip. "It's xenaphobic to exclude forest animals. Why can't they all live here with us, like Rags and Oliver?"

Shep tried to explain so the youngster could understand. "You've lived a sheltered life here, Pip. You don't understand that some animals prey on the small and weak. They eat chickens and ducks—and even cows and sheep, if they're large and fierce enough. They're too wild and violent to live here on the farm with us."

"That's stereotyping," Pip objected. "It's unfair to condemn all bears for the actions of a few. The Professor says that the forest is a place of peace. Animals live in happy co-existence there, maintaining the balance of nature. It's the fences that introduce violence. If we didn't build and maintain them, we'd all be part of the same big ecosystem, living in harmony with our surroundings, like birds and fish."

"I prefer the balance on the farm," replied Shep, "where the big ones don't eat the small ones, and we work together and help each other survive. We're farm animals, Pip, with rights and obligations. We live by the law, not the wild ways that rule out there."

"I don't want to be a farm animal," sulked Pip, slowing his trot till he fell behind.

Shep stopped in his tracks and turned to face his son.

"Look, Pip, your Uncle Duke wasn't born here on the farm. He was a stray. He got separated from a hunter and survived for weeks out there in the woods, lost and alone. When he finally staggered up to our fence, he was almost dead from hunger. Though he was a stranger, we let him stay because his mind knew tameness.

"It's not because they live in the forest that we keep the wild ones out," Shep concluded, "but because they walk a different path than ours. If we let them on the farm, nothing would be safe."

"That's so parochial," mumbled Pip. "The Professor says that we should all think and act like world citizens, not selfishly hoard our privileges to ourselves."

Shep didn't know what "parochial" meant and so couldn't argue the point, but it sounded wrong to his way of thinking. What was more natural than farm animals keeping out predators? Without the farm they'd have no food or privileges. He didn't know what was going on over there at that new school, but tomorrow he was going to sneak over and have a look.

The next morning, Shep crept over to the orchard and ducked behind a bush to observe Pip's morning class. Oliver was supposed to be instructing the young in the art of apple picking, but, oddly, no one was in the trees. Instead the students were gathered around in a circle, listening to the possum talk as he paced back and forth on the furrowed ground.

Shep pricked up his ears to catch his words on the breeze.

"This orchard was once the site of a great injustice," said Oliver, pounding a palm with his little fist. "There was a time when the forest animals who came here were considered wild and unteachable and driven off or killed. They weren't allowed so much as to step onto the farm. They could only stare at the fruit in the treetops, from behind that fence there, dreaming of the day when they too could enjoy the bounty of nature.

"But the horses and cattle didn't believe in social justice," he said, suddenly stopping and staring at the young faces before him. "They were large, powerful beasts who believed in the principle that might makes right. If an innocent woodland creature tried to scurry across and nibble a forbidden apple, a giant hoof would mercilessly crush him to the ground. He'd be pounded into dust in a frenzy of violence and hatred.

"That's what I think about when I pick fruit," the possum said with a nod toward the treetop. "You see, I was one of the excluded myself. I didn't enjoy the special privileges that come with unjust power. I was one of the downtrodden—not like you: spoiled children who have the fruit brought right to their beds."

The possum stared down at an anxious little hen. "It's your hunger and greed that kept us possums down," he said. "It's what still keeps us at the margins of society. Think of that every time you eat a pear or apple. Think what your privilege did to us innocents.

"That's why," he said more firmly, "no matter what subject you're studying here in school, your first thought should always be, 'How can I advance the cause of social justice?' If you don't make social justice your first concern, you'll never be a proper citizen—or, need I say it, ever pass this course."

The possum smiled. "Any questions?" he asked, his black eyes shining like polished beads.

Most of the students simply hung their heads and looked at the ground, or stared past each other, avoiding the possum's eyes. They seemed too embarrassed to insult their teacher with questions—till Bronson, the half-grown pig, lifted his snout and asked, "Uh, how exactly are we supposed to pick fruit that's out of our reach? I can't even stretch my head up to the lowest branch—much less climb."

The possum smiled facetiously at the pig.

"You can't reach the fruit," he said, "because your species hasn't evolved as far as us possums and raccoons. You don't have hands—just those possum-stomping black hooves appropriate to your kind. You're earth creatures, not sky creatures like me and Rags. You're the burden we fruit-picking kind have to bear every day of our lives. We feed you with our labor, and you look down your snouts at us. That's what I want you all to think about till tomorrow when the class meets again.

"Class dismissed," he called over the shuffle of departing feet. "Tomorrow I want each of you to give a two-minute talk on the social justice of apple picking."

CHAPTER 24

A light snow fell over the gray, empty fields, signaling the onset of winter. It dusted the roofs of the barn, henhouse, and stables, and glittered on the ground as the sun half hid behind a bank of clouds.

Freed from their studies till spring, the delirious students spent the morning skittering over the snow sheet, sliding and chasing each other on wobbly legs or carving crude hearts into the crust to impress their future mates.

Later in the afternoon, the students gathered outside the barn for their last instructions from Olivia, the new pageant director. She coached them how to project their voices and where to stand, encouraging the shy ones to stand up straight and showing the others how to accompany their lines with dramatic gestures.

Leaning against a fence post, Gertrude waited for the play to begin, feeling relaxed for the first time in weeks. Since school began, all she'd heard were complaints. The older citizens complained that the school was filling their youngsters' heads with new ideas, and the newer citizens complained that their young were too often punished for misbehavior. The pageant would be the perfect balm to soothe the hurt feelings of both. It would show the sacrifice, wisdom, and courage of the farm's founders and demonstrate to the new immigrants what it meant to be a citizen of the farm.

Gert leaned forward as Olivia stepped onto the makeshift stage to thunderous stamps and shouts.

Then the crowd grew quiet again as a young possum took center stage to declaim his opening line.

Gert's heart rose with the familiar cadences of her own inspired prose:

"This is how the animals of Green Pastures Farm became free and self-governing citizens. . . ."

She closed her eyes and let the sounds wash over her like warm summer rain.

But after the opening cadences, the tune turned sour and discordant as the possum abandoned her script. The courage and ingenuity shown by the animals in mastering the difficult art of farming were passed over in a few terse lines. Not a word was said about forming the Animal Council. As the possum described it, the farm was a backward place, sunk in ignorance and fear.

Gert stood up straight and glared toward the distant stage.

Now the possum was finished, and a young raccoon replaced him at center stage.

"Then out of the silent shadows of the forest, a stranger came," shouted the raccoon. "But instead of a warm welcome, the poor creature was greeted by the clamor of war alarms.

"'It's a bear!' cried the sheep. 'Sound the tocsin. Call the cows and horses to war. A trespasser has come to invade our peaceful farm.'"

At last, thought Gertrude. *Here comes our glorious triumph over the bear. At least they've got that right.*

Gert smiled as the story rose toward its thrilling climax.

" . . . The dogs and cattle and pigs came running to the pasture, where they formed a living battlement of hooves and teeth and horns. Only one voice was raised above the clamor of war to counsel peace. A brave duck named Pierre resisted the prejudice of his neighbors to argue in favor of reason and tolerance."

"But his fellow citizens were blinded by rage and hate," said a young lamb, pressing forward into the limelight. "They refused to break the endless cycle of violence. Pushing the duck to the rear, they advanced against the bear without warning. The dogs snapped at his flanks, and the cattle lowered their horns and advanced like a ring of spears.

"Outnumbered and encircled, the poor bear was nearly trapped when a giant stallion rose up and struck at him with flashing hooves."

"Without even trying to understand the bear's perspective," clucked a young hen, stepping forward to replace the lamb, "the farm animals drove away their unoffending guest. With blows and curses, they sent him reeling back into the forest to lick his wounds, rejected and alone. Whatever wisdom he might have shared with them was lost—along with any hope of understanding between species."

The hen stepped back and bowed low to the ground. Then Tooth, the half-grown beaver, stepped up and hoarsely cried, "The terrifying specter of the bear was gone, but not the shadow cast over the animals' hearts and minds. Larger and fiercer than any bear, the shadow of *xenaphobia* stalked Green Pastures Farm, looking for souls to devour."

The beaver retreated to the shadows. Then a half-grown gosling opened her bill and let loose a ringing cry:

"But then a heroic deer named Xena stepped onto the scene!"

As the gosling spoke, a young doe stepped through the chorus line and limped across the stage with imagined pain.

"Wounded and ailing, the deer leapt the fence of hostility that surrounded the farm and conquered its citizens with her gentle ways. She forced the animals to confront the judgmentalism that blinded their eyes and hardened their hearts against her. She showed them that a deer could be their friend and equal. She blazed a pathway for her fellow forest creatures, so they too could follow the path of domesticity and enjoy the freely given bounty of mother earth."

"Other heroes followed in Xena's steps," proclaimed a calf, stepping up beside the doe. "And the farm grew rich and prosperous. With the help of a brave family of raccoons, they harvested endless crates of ripe fruit. Then possums came and lent their hands to the effort, increasing the farm's harvest of trust and tolerance."

At this point a young raccoon crept forward, covered with coal dust. To complete his disguise, two strips of wood protruded from beneath his upper lip, like giant teeth. The crowd laughed at his resemblance to a beaver.

"When their fence broke down," the gosling said, patting the raccoon's head and sending up puffs of coal dust, "the farm turned once again to the forest for help. To their rescue came this humble, helpful beaver.

"The beaver fixed their fence and became a lifelong friend. Now the farm sleeps safely at night behind his handiwork. The fence binds the farm and forest together in trust and friendship."

At a signal from the director, the whole chorus stepped forward and recited their lines in unison.

"Here we stand now, a farm full of diverse species living together in peace. The new covenant of Biodiversity has rebuilt the farm's foundation and made it firm. Together we will guard against intolerance and hate. We will build a fence around our thoughts to stop the dark specter of xenaphobia. We will post sentinels at our teeth to hold back hurtful words. Green Pastures Farm is not built on laws and customs, but on the idea that housecat and cougar, grizzly and billy goat, heron and hen are all brothers and sisters beneath their skin or feathers."

Now abandoning her role of director, Olivia stepped forward and delivered the final soliloquy, moving her little hands in time with its rhythms like a conductor.

"The fence that surrounds the farm is a bridge and a ladder.

"We cross it to find our better selves.

"We climb it to reach higher stages of understanding. . . ."

The nauseating speech went on, but Gertrude turned and fled in a flutter of wings toward the empty barn. She wanted to stretch her mighty pinions and fly somewhere far, far away—to some Southern tropical paradise . . . or maybe all the way to the South Pole. She didn't care. So long as she never had to hear an "I-told-you-so" or look into the stricken faces of her friends.

CHAPTER 25

As they gathered in the barn, the leading citizens of Green Pastures Farm fumed at the way the pageant portrayed their heroic history—none more than Kit and his harem of irate mares.

"Didn't you hear what they said about me?" Kit asked, glaring at Gert. "They made it sound as if the bear had come to give us a bouquet of wild flowers. They made it look like *I* was the one who threatened our peace. You run the school. It's your responsibility to see that nothing like this ever happens again."

"The way those yearlings described it," sniffed Mara, "the most heroic action that ever took place on this farm was the trespass of a sick deer."

She snorted derisively. "As if nearly bleeding to death on someone else's property were the highest act of courage. What about how we learned to farm without hands?"

Gertrude explained for the tenth time that she hadn't approved Olivia's play, but had instead urged her to stick to last year's script. She pleaded for another chance to make things right. Some of the Council members were already grumbling about dismissing her from her job as superintendent. Luckily, Kit was the Chief Executive and had the last word. After a few more grumbles and snorts, he decided simply to put her on probation.

"But the next time something like this happens," he warned, "you're out. We'll turn the school over to someone more reliable."

Relieved to escape with her job and some remnant of her dignity, Gert returned to her duties with a renewed sense of purpose. She'd had it with unruly students. It was time to crack down on the little miscreants. As for her freewheeling teachers, she'd talk to them and make them toe the line. From now on, she'd watch over the school like a hawk and make an example of the first upstart that challenged her authority.

On her way to the orchard the next morning to talk to Oliver about his apple-picking class, Gertrude spied a group of truant raccoons and possums. They were hiding in a patch of weeds beside a rain barrel. Marching right up to them, she grabbed the nearest possum by the ear and gave him a nasty shake.

"What are you doing out of class?" she demanded. "You're supposed to be over in the orchard learning to pick."

"Aw, leave off," muttered the possum. "You better let go of my ear."

"What about you?" Gert demanded of a grinning raccoon. "Shouldn't you be in the Professor's seminar? What are you doing out here, standing around looking down at that, that . . ."

"Egg!"

Gert stared down at the shattered remains of several eggshells.

"You've, you've been poaching!" shouted the goose. "You little thieves. You wild unpredictable little savages . . ."

In a flash, Gert remembered Hetty's complaint that eggs had been disappearing from the bucket. Gert had to admit, the haul seemed a bit lighter of late. These eggshells answered a lot of nagging questions.

"Who you calling a savage?" sneered young Oscar, now that his ear was free. "If I was a big ugly bird like you, I'd be careful who I insulted."

"We never touched those eggs," said the raccoon. "Those shells were on the ground when we got here. Probably some stinky dog stole them. They're the only ones who eat eggs around here."

"You've got egg in your fur," said Gert, pointing at the raccoon's shiny muzzle. "Right there, around your whiskers.

"Wild beasts," she muttered under her breath. "No trespassing. No trespassing. That's how it should be around here."

In a fit of rage, she reached out and grabbed the raccoon's ear with her horny bill and gave it a vicious shake. Her first thought was to march the little hooligan over to his mother and let her deal with him. Then she decided it would be much better to take him before the Council.

"Ouch," said the raccoon. "Let go of my ear, or I'll wring your scrawny neck."

With a quick dodge, the raccoon ducked under her bill and grasped Gert's long white neck with his two front paws.

Just as her throat pinched tight, a low voice growled from behind, "Let go. Let go or I'll bite that paw off at the wrist."

Gert staggered from the raccoon's grasp, gulping for air.

When her vision cleared, she saw that Jessy had already backed her attacker up against the rain barrel. With teeth bared and shackles raised, she looked like she meant business.

"That dog don't look so big to me," sneered Oscar, with a quick glance at his friends. "We could take her if we wanted. If she snaps at Little Rags, I say we go for her throat."

"Try it," said Jessy. "But then my mate and Duke over there will hear the ruckus and come down on you like thunderbolts. By the time we get through with you, there'll be nothing left but fur and toenails."

"Aw, we didn't mean nothin'," said Little Rags, backing away. "What are you getting so worked up about? We were only joking."

With some help from Gert, Jessy marched the truants over to the barn and locked them in an empty stall, to deal with later.

But before they'd even left the barn, the prisoners had climbed from the stall and escaped. Without so much as a whisper, they skittered across the barnyard toward the fence where the Professor was teaching his class.

With Hetty's help, Gert rallied a group of angry hens and took her case against the egg thieves to the Council. But as soon as she entered the barn, she discovered that she'd been too slow. The students had already gotten there ahead of her, with a counter-suit of their own.

"What do you mean I've been accused of violating the rights of students?" she asked indignantly of Emma. "I'm here to charge four students with stealing. I have witnesses," she added, twisting her neck to look for Jessy in the crowd.

She spied the little border collie standing next to May and Mara and sighed relief.

"The students have already admitted to damaging eggs," said Duke, in his role of sergeant at arms. "We're here about another matter."

"You don't think I took the eggs, do you?" asked Gert with a laugh. "I'm a goose, for heaven's sake. Why on earth would I steal eggs?"

"We're not here about eggs," said Kit, staring down from his place at the head of the Council. "It's much more serious than that. You've been charged with violating the constitution and harassing students."

"Harassing students?" laughed Gert. "That's rich. I caught those little savages eating eggs."

"Don't say anything else," whispered Shep. "Let me do the talking."

"Let the Council note that the defendant just called her fellow citizens 'savages,'" said the Professor, stepping up to Ike, the presiding judge.

"Savages," the owl repeated, then turned and glared at Gert.

"Duly noted," said Ike. "Ahem."

"They stole those eggs," asserted Gertrude. "I don't see what this has to do with the constitution."

"As I already stipulated to the court," said the Professor, cutting in, "the students have admitted to mishandling eggs. That's a separate matter. We're here to inquire about gross violation of these young citizens' rights."

Gert couldn't believe her eyes. The three guilty students were staring down at her from the witness stand with obvious glee at her predicament.

"According to their previous testimony," said the Professor, suddenly turning to interrogate Gert, "you called these young citizens 'wild.' Is that true?"

"Yes, I called them wild. That's just how they were acting. That raccoon there had egg all over his chin."

"Three of the students in question have already testified that the raccoon got the egg on his chin while cleaning up the mess after accidentally dropping them. That's not an issue."

The barn owl looked at Gert.

"By your own admission, you have accused these citizens of being wild. Did you not also accuse them unfairly of being trespassers?"

The Professor blinked his large dark fathomless eyes.

"I may have said something about trespassers," admitted Gert. "So what? They *were* trespassers not that long ago. I was only telling the truth."

"So you refuse to recognize the legal rights of these four young citizens?" the Professor asked. "Instead, you slander them even now, refusing to acknowledge their legal right to be on the farm. You refuse to admit that they walk on level ground with you. You deny them the same right to a voice and an ear granted to every citizen of Green Pastures Farm by the constitution."

"Look," said Gert angrily. "I see what you're doing. You've got a couple of thieves over there who've been snatching eggs and eating them on the sly, and you're changing the subject to something I might have said in a moment of anger when I caught them at their business."

Gert turned to the group of angry hens she'd brought to bolster her case.

"Go ahead," she demanded, "ask these chickens here why the bucket's been so light lately. Ask the pigs and dogs if their breakfast is as big as it used to be. Someone's been stealing eggs, and we all know who."

Before the Professor could ask another question, Shep stepped forward and addressed the court.

"I'd like to ask Hetty to step up here and speak to what Gert just said. Come on, Hetty, tell us, What has been happening to the eggs?"

"W-well," stuttered Hetty, looking nervously about, "I can't say for sure, but some of us in the henhouse think all of the eggs aren't making it over to the barn. There are a lot of possums hanging about the coop these days. Some say they have a natural taste for eggs. I sure do notice them staring at them a lot. Seems like more than a casual interest, if you know what I mean."

The Professor smiled, then paced back and forth before the hen, unsettling her even more with his silent pacing.

By the time he turned to ask another question, Hetty was almost twitching with anxiety. Gertrude suddenly regretted relying on hens for support. They were notoriously skittish and tended to lose their heads in a crisis.

Suddenly the barn owl stopped pacing and asked almost soothingly, "Hetty, are you afraid of possums?"

"C-certainly," stuttered Hetty, eyes darting wildly about. "Of course. We're not used to them in the henhouse. They're sneaky-like. And they have those wicked little teeth, like needles, almost made for piercing eggs."

The Professor stared long and hard at the witness, further stoking her anxiety.

"And do the other hens also fear the presence of possums and raccoons in the house you share?"

"Sure. We all do. How can we trust them, the way they stare at us sometimes? It's like they're sizing us up for a meal."

The Professor turned and gazed at the judge, then at the Council, then, with a sudden twist of his head, at the assembly behind him.

"One last question," he said, turning back to Hetty. "When hens are nervous, does that affect their ability to lay eggs?"

"C-certainly," Hetty stuttered. "You think it's easy pushing those things out when every muscle in your body is tied in knots?"

"So," said the owl, "what has most likely affected egg production in recent days is not theft, but your own suspicion and fear? In a word, your own fear of the possums' otherness—isn't that true?"

A disapproving murmur rippled through the crowd.

"In short, Miss Hetty," said the owl, turning to face the assembly, "you suffer from an acute case of xenophobia, isn't that right?"

"Xenaphobia," bleated a chorus of angry sheep.

"Xenaphobia," chanted the students who'd come to see the bossy goose on trial.

"Order," demanded Kit with a stamp of his giant hoof. "This room will come to order immediately."

As the chanting died down, he glared down past the witness and prosecutor at Gertrude. Then after a few whispered exchanges with the other Council members, he stamped his hoof again and addressed the goose.

"Gertrude, it's clear that you—and your principal witness—bear an unhealthy prejudice against these young animals. Regardless of the merits of your charge, your own words prove that you have not walked on the same level ground as your fellow citizens. You have denied them the rights and privileges granted to all citizens of Green Pastures Farm. You are unworthy to direct a school whose mission is to educate young minds in the ways of tameness.

"As Chief Executive, I hereby relieve you of your position of superintendent. Tomorrow the Council will meet to decide on a new one. Until then, this meeting is dismissed. The Council will decide tomorrow what to do with you."

CHAPTER 26

In the days after Gert's disgrace, a cold blast swept down from the north, freezing the puddles and ponds and forcing even the hardiest animals indoors. As the wind howled outside, Gert nursed her hurt feelings in the company of her friends and neighbors in the crowded barn.

Thanks to the Professor, her punishment had been reduced to something called "Sensitivity Training" in next spring's "orientation." She didn't know exactly what those words meant, but she was happy that the punishment had been postponed till a later season. In the meantime, to keep herself busy, she took charge of getting the barn ready for the annual Winter Festival.

While Shep organized a work party to set up the crèche in the barn, she filled the empty spaces with hay bales so all the new citizens would have a place to hear Ike's sermon. The story of the spirit-shepherd never failed to fill hearts with joy and reverence. This year, she hoped the new citizens would be inspired to make their own pilgrimages toward tameness.

But by the time the great day arrived, the cold had driven most of the new citizens into hiding. Some went underground. Others hid beneath the floor boards or deep in the hearts of wood-piles. Though it pleased Gert to see their numbers diminish, she regretted that so few remained to be swayed by Ike's eloquence.

When the moment finally came, only a handful of shivering possums and others remained to hear the old ram speak. Arriving late, Ike got off to a bad start, stumbling over long words and sometimes losing his place. He seemed to have less energy and passion than in past years.

Each time he paused to take a labored breath, Gert glanced over to gauge the new citizens' reaction. She was disappointed that most looked bored and ill at ease.

At the sermon's conclusion, a reverential hush descended over the barn. Then a small voice broke the silence.

"Where are all the possums and raccoons?" it asked.

As everyone looked toward the crèche to see who'd spoken, Gert spotted a young possum eyeing the figurines.

"Yeah," piped up a deeper voice. "How come you got eight sheep but not a single beaver?"

A quail walked up to the crèche and slipped among its silent figures, surveying them with a narrow eye.

"What's that thing there?" she asked, pointing at a camel. "It looks like a long-legged, hump-backed cow. How come you have that monstrosity, but not one quail? Looks like this so-called spirit-shepherd favors hoofed creatures."

"That's breedism," muttered a possum. "Pure and simple."

"I see where this is coming from," added a ferret and vanished into a crack between the floorboards.

"It's insensitive is what it is," added a groundhog. "I don't mind telling you, I feel completely excluded."

"You're missing the point," called out Gertrude. "We're all represented here. These figures show that, symbolically, we're all called to walk the path of tameness, whatever our species. There are no geese either, see? The little barn can't include every creature on earth."

"Looks like you got a lot of farm animals in there," called a voice from the rear. "I don't see any forest-born, unless you count that hump-backed thing."

Maybe that's because farm animals are tame and forest animals aren't, Gert nearly shouted.

But recent experience had taught her to hold her tongue. The cold was already driving them underground. Better be grateful, she thought, for a few weeks of relative peace.

The lethargy Ike showed throughout his sermon proved to be far more serious than anyone knew. Two days later, he collapsed on a pile of straw and coughed up blood. For three days, he slipped in and out of sleep, then lapsed into a coma and died one night after his watchers had fallen asleep.

His funeral was the saddest occasion in memory. After a moving elegy delivered by Eudora, his dearest friend, the animals buried the old ram near the garden beside Grover. When the horses finally lowered him into the ground, Shep nearly collapsed with grief. Later, when everyone else was asleep, Duke filled the night with despondent howls and wails. For days afterward, the animals were nearly stupefied by despair. Some couldn't even complete their daily chores.

Ike's death also left them with an immediate problem. Who was going to assume his position as Supreme Judge?

As Chief Executive, Kit had the duty of appointing Ike's replacement, but he refused to make a choice until he'd consulted representatives of each of the five houses and considered every possible candidate. After days of silent deliberations, he appeared to have narrowed the choice to Eudora or Shep. Then one day the Professor proposed that Kit appoint one of the new citizens and the whole farm fell to debating his suggestion.

"It's time we had some new blood," said young Bronson. "Ike was a fine old ram, but it's time we looked past the old-school folks to someone more in step with the times. A lot of things have changed since Ike's day. Eudora's too old, and Shep has too many other things to do on the farm. Kit should pick someone new."

"What the Professor said is right," offered Olivia. "It would show good faith for Kit to appoint a new citizen as judge. Many of us feel excluded by this place. I think he should give us possums some special consideration."

"This isn't a popularity contest," countered Raymond. "A judge has got to understand the law."

"And we don't?" asked Olivia. "What, you think only dogs and cows can understand? What do you think we've been studying all these weeks in school? The Professor taught me more law than some of these farm animals ever learned. I know more law than that dumb Duke. Just cause he's big don't mean he's got a lot of sense. Maybe Shep is as smart as you all think, but it ain't fair to pick another farm animal to be the judge. I say Kit should pick a raccoon or possum."

"A possum?" snorted Duke. "That's just what we need. I think old Shep is the right dog for the job."

"Dog is right," said Oscar. "There are four dogs on this farm, counting Pip. Four. Olivia's right. The last thing we need is a dog interpreting the law for the whole farm. Take a look around sometime. We possums are severely underrepresented."

"Underrepresented?" scoffed Barlow. "That's rich. You've completely taken over the pigpen."

"So why are you still calling it the pigpen?" sneered Oscar. "Looks to me like you're still trying to hang on to your special privileges."

"How about I come over there and hang on to your skinny neck?" asked Barlow, advancing toward him.

"That's right, try to bully me, you fat pig. This is just exactly what I'm talking about. If we don't get some representation in the system here, you and your kind are going to bully us forever."

Kit finally intervened to stop the bickering.

"All right," he said. "In all fairness, we've got some divisions here. Maybe it's time to pick a reconciliation candidate. I've just made up my mind. I'm going to appoint Rags to be judge. He's been studying the law since the day he became a citizen. And no one works harder to make the farm a success. He's held citizenship here longer than any of the new arrivals. And his appointment will show all the others that here on Green Pastures Farm the law means what it says. We walk on level ground, every one of us, whether on hoof, paw, web, or claw.

"I hereby appoint Rags to the position of Supreme Judge," he announced with a snort. "I know he'll honor the law and all of us.

"That's it," he said, banging his hoof. "I've made my appointment."

CHAPTER 27

After an unusually cold winter, spring drifted in on a warm wind from the south, bringing robins and rain. Within days, the pastures were covered with a thick carpet of grass. Daffodils bloomed along creeks, and the wet fields were primed for planting. Soon every hoof and beak on the farm was busy poking holes in the wet earth, dropping in seeds, and covering them over with rich brown soil.

Yawning and stretching, animals arose from hibernation and stumbled into the light of day. Soon the fields swarmed with possums and raccoons dragging seed sacks over the furrows behind horses and cows. Groundhogs appeared next and were immediately put to work tending the vegetable gardens. Their powerful paws could part the earth like trowels. They had a marvelous instinct for coaxing green sprouts and shoots from the fertile soil and stood guard over the unfolding blossoms like mother hens.

No one seemed to notice the steady stream of weasels, squirrels, muskrats, and chipmunks that flowed over the fences and infiltrated the work gangs so long as they lightened the animals' loads and made work go quicker.

Shep saw that it was futile to try and staunch the brimming tide, so the dogs stopped patrolling the fences and spent their time instead policing the fields and buildings, where new troubles broke out daily.

The sheep complained that Buck, the young son of Xena, was bullying them in the pasture. Using his antlers to intimidate the ewes and lambs, he threatened to drive out any sheep who disobeyed him. In the midst of a food shortage, he kept the best shoots for himself and a few wild friends who leapt the fence to share the booty by night. Shep had talked to Buck twice already, but the young deer had scoffed at his warnings. Shep told him if he didn't toe the line, he'd have to bring him up before the judge.

Tensions were rising all across the farm as food supplies ran low and bellies felt the bony pinch of hunger. The increased population had drained their winter stores. All that was left to eat was some unused seed grain. Despite having planted a record number of acres, they had to survive on quarter rations till their crops came in.

The possums took their own steps to deal with the problem by calling a special meeting in the pigpen.

"I'm hungry," said Oscar. "I don't see why the pigs get to have a special bucket every morning just for them. I say it's time we split the eggs and milk and whatever else is in there among us all—equal shares."

"But we're pigs," objected Barlow. "I'm bigger than twenty of you possums. We can't survive on a fraction of our morning meal."

"Your days of privilege are over, Porky. Hooves and paws walk on the same ground, remember? Or haven't you heard of that little thing called a constitution?"

"You're distorting its meaning," replied Bertha. "We walk on the same level ground, sure, but that doesn't mean we all have to eat the same amount of food. Horses are bigger than hens. That's just common sense. It's the same with pigs and possums. We need more to eat than you."

"Well, that just works out fine for you big animals, don't it," chipped in Oscar. "Too bad for you the constitution says otherwise. One voice, one vote. I say it's time to put the proposal on the table."

"Too bad you're not a horse," quipped Omar, casting a grin at Barlow. "Then you could eat all the grass you want. You think it's fair that the horses and sheep get to fill up on grass while we're splitting sunflower seeds over here?"

"Why don't you vote to eat the grass then?" muttered Barlow. "What's the matter, you don't like roughage?"

"Keep talking, Porky, and we'll vote to expel you from the Possum Pen. You're only here thanks to our generosity. Remember that."

"You call me Porky again," growled Barlow, "and I'll be eating possum stew some dark moonless night. You scrawny little marsupial mutant, I've eaten pumpkins bigger than you."

"You watch that 'marsupial mutant' talk, fat boy, or I'll bring you up on harassment charges. You'll be taking classes over there with little Miss Gertrude in the barnyard, if you don't watch out."

"'Do not kill,'" chipped in Oscar. "What's the matter, Barlow, you forget your own sacred laws? Or maybe you just believe what's convenient."

He turned to Olive. "Okay, I move we split the morning bucket, equal shares. All in favor?"

The motion passed with only two dissenting votes. Bronson voted with the triumphant possums. It served his parents right for giving him the job of carrying buckets in the first place, he thought. The change would hurt them more than him. The possums had already promised him an extra share for not reporting them for stealing eggs. Lately, Oscar, Omar, and Little Rags were only too happy to help him over in the henhouse. The eggs were good eating. Since helping him gather eggs, the three thieves had grown fat and lazy by bribing the leaders of work gangs to let them off early. Now they rarely worked beyond mid-morning in the fields. Bronson looked forward to the day when he too could skip out early on work details.

As their stores diminished and the farm's population increased, the food shortage worsened. Two weeks before the first apple harvest, stomachs were starting to howl. Kit called an emergency meeting of the Council to deal with the deepening crisis. Since the weather was mild and their numbers now exceeded the barn's capacity, the meeting was held outdoors in the open air.

"We've come here today to decide how to deal with the food shortage," Kit began. "We have to plan for the coming days. It's already mating season. We have to consider our future resources and decide how many more animals the farm can support. The first thing we might want to think about is curbing the number of refugees we take in from the forest. . . ."

"Why is it that the first thing you ever think about is how to reduce the number of forest-born?" asked Oliver. "It's pure xenaphobia, that's what it is."

"Xenaphobia," bleated the sheep. "Xenaphobia! Xenaphobia!"

"Order," shouted Kit, stamping his hoof and flaring his nostrils. "Everyone will have a turn to speak."

The crowd stopped chanting and waited for a speaker to be recognized by the chair.

Barlow was the first to catch the stallion's attention.

"The thing is," said the pig, "if we all have bigger litters this year, we'll starve—unless we cut back on the trespassing."

"Trespassing!" shouted a weasel. "Since when is our legitimate right to work on this farm trespassing? Thanks to our help, this will be the biggest crop the farm has ever seen. It's not a weasel's nature to plant seeds, but we're out there every morning pulling our weight so you can eat corn this fall. Oliver's right, anyone who wants to stop us weasels and possums from coming onto the farm is nothing but a breedist."

"Whatever happened to Many-Animalism?" Emma asked gently, with a glance at the other sheep. "Hoof, web, paw, claw, remember? We're all in this together."

"Look, last year was a bad year," continued Barlow. "Only one piglet survived from our litter, and Pip was the only one who came through for Jessy and Shep. Gertrude had only seven eggs last summer—"

"Eight!" shouted Gertrude.

"—and overall we had fewer offspring across the farm. If we have more this year, added to the constant influx of forest animals, we'll soon be overrun. Possums have something like sixteen per litter. If we don't cut back, we'll be up to our eyeballs in possums by August."

"Xenaphobia, xenaphobia," bleated the sheep.

Their chant was soon joined by a chorus of angry possums and raccoons.

"Order!" shouted Kit over the rising din. This time it took several minutes for it to grow quiet enough for the debate to resume.

"If there's overpopulation," called out a groundhog, "then the farm animals can reduce their litters. There's more of you than us. It's breedism to single us out for exclusion.

"And another thing," called out a chipmunk. "Aren't there supposed to be elections? We chipmunks have been working hard for weeks, and there's no one to represent our views. Why can't we have a chipmunk on the Council? It's only fair."

"The elections are scheduled for the week after planting," said Kit. "It's always the same every year."

"But what about cutting back on your litters?" asked Tooth. "If you really believe in Many-Animalism like you say, you should cut back and give us a chance to get even with you."

Kit frowned at the young beaver.

"We'll leave that to the discretion of each couple," he said. "We're good-hearted animals here on Green Pastures Farm. I have faith that we'll all do the right thing."

CHAPTER 28

Gertrude was surprised to see Shep and Barlow among the students in her Sensitivity class. The Professor was conducting the class himself, assisted by Rags, the new judge, and Olive, the possum who'd just been elected to represent the Possum Pen.

The three farm animals were by far the largest and oldest members of the class. They were surrounded by dozens of chicks, possums, young lambs, groundhogs, calves, and a few scattered weasels and squirrels who were gathered here for Orientation.

"What are you in for?" Gert joked, turning to Shep.

The border collie looked quite downcast at being treated like a yearling pup.

"Something called profiling, or stereotyping," replied Shep. "I'm not sure. It's all because I stopped some groundhogs from sneaking under the fence. They said the only reason I stopped them was because they were groundhogs. Well, I couldn't argue with that. Seems like if we're going to have vegetables to eat, we might want to keep wild groundhogs off the farm. But Kit says it's wrong to stop animals just because they belong to a certain species. So he ordered me to take this class."

"What about you?" Gert asked, turning to Barlow.

The pig frowned, multiplying chins.

"I called a possum some names," he confessed with a crooked grin. He looked around at the jostling students and muttered, "How long do you think we have to stay here? I hope they're serving lunch because I haven't eaten a thing this morning."

His stomach growled as if to underscore his point.

"Hey, look," he said, thrusting his snout over Shep's shoulder. "Here comes Raymond."

The rooster spied his three friends and strutted over to join them. In answer to Gert's question, he explained what had brought him here.

"I got elected to represent the chicken coop," he said. "That Miss Gray thought she had it in the bag. All the hens are scared to death of her. She made sure all of the resident possums—and even a few ferrets from under the floor—were there to vote, but when the ballots were counted, I won. Only six hens voted for the raccoon. Next thing you know, I'm back on the top roost again."

The rooster puffed out his chest feathers.

"See, the hens have lost so many eggs, they're getting suspicious of everyone. And now with their chicks running about, they decided I was the best one to protect them. That Miss Gray tried to bully the hens into voting for her. She thought she could lean on me, too, but you know what? I told her to back off or I'd tear out her eye, and by heaven she hasn't gotten close enough to risk a good scratch ever since."

The rooster straightened his back and plumped up his blood-red comb.

"I told you all this novelty would wear off. Things will be right again soon. Just wait."

"Eh, you're not taking this class because you got elected to the Council," Gert said. "I asked why you're here."

"Oh, that," Raymond said. "One of the possums said that if I didn't accept their way of doing things, I'd face 'wild justice.' I said that's just what I expected from a bunch of wild possums, and the next thing I knew I was found guilty of offensive speech. I hope the Professor explains why threatening me is okay but calling those possums 'wild' got me sentenced to two weeks of sunrise detention."

After another minute of noisy bustling, the students began to settle down. The Professor, perched on a fence at the head of the class, drew their attention with the clang of an old cowbell.

"Look around you," said the Professor, once the students had grown quiet. "We're here to celebrate biodiversity on this first day of orientation.

"To get things started, I want to begin with a simple exercise."

He beamed at the sea of attentive young faces.

"First, I'd like all of the animals who have ever heard themselves referred to as trespassers to please sit down on the ground. That's right, sit right down there where you are in the dirt."

All of the animals sat down except the four adults and all of the young farm animals.

"Now," said the Professor, "I'd like all of those animals who have never said the word *trespasser* also to sit down."

All of the young farm animals crouched down on their bellies, leaving Gert, Raymond, Shep, and Barlow standing.

"There, look around you," said the Professor. "Look and see who's standing and who's sitting down."

All eyes turned toward Gert and her trio of friends.

"I'd like all of you sitting down now to think of a question you'd like to ask the four animals standing. Take your time. Soon as you have one, please stand and address your questions to one of them."

At first there was much head scratching and awkward silence.

Finally, one of the young weasels stood up and, turning to Barlow, asked, "Why do you say such hurtful things? What did we ever do for you to call us trespassers?"

Barlow hemmed and hawed, then looked desperately toward Shep for guidance.

"I, I didn't know it was hurtful," he stammered. "I guess I called you trespassers because here on the farm all of us are tame, and you're all, well, wild."

The pig's speech was met by a howl of angry protests.

"Who you calling wild?" shouted a beaver.

"That's breedism," barked a young fox.

The Professor had to ring his bell for a long time before the shouting diminished enough for him to be heard again.

"All right," said the Professor over dying protests. "Tell the four animals standing what it feels like to be called 'wild.'"

"What would that fat pig care?" asked a possum, sulking. "He's been pampered his whole life on this farm. All he's ever known is the privilege of being a domesticated pig."

"It hurts, that's how it feels," said a groundhog. "Anyway, how would he know how it feels to be an animal? He's not one himself; he's a manimal—animal on the outside, human on the inside. He'd never survive in the forest. He needs us so-called trespassers to keep him fed and pampered right here."

"How do you like it, pork chop?" shouted a voice from the rear. "How you like being kicked off your throne and told what you are, pig?"

"Wait a minute," interjected Shep. "This is uncalled for. Barlow has the right to say what he wants. Every animal has a voice and an ear, remember? It's not fair to gang up on him like that. What gives you the right to call him names?"

"What comes around goes around," hissed a mottled green snake. "You call us trespassers. We just say what you are—pigs and dogs. You're just upset because you lost your privileged status."

"Shep's right," protested Gert. "We geese have a saying: what's good for the goose is good for the gander. If you don't like being called names, then don't call us names either. That's only fair."

"One voice, one ear, eh?" said Olive. The possum cast a knowing look at the Professor.

"The law is just a mask to protect your privileged status. You've never been called a trespasser, so you think it's your right to say whatever you want. That's why you're here: to learn that your speech is offensive. Some things cause so much hurt that they can't be said."

"Look," Raymond interjected, "someone just called Barlow 'pork chop.' I find that offensive too."

"What you find offensive don't matter," said Olive. She turned to the barn owl on the fence beside her. "Isn't that right, Professor?"

"Well, yes," the owl said. "It's not the same thing to be called a name if you've never experienced exclusion. But if you've been excluded, offensive words amount to violent actions. And so a different standard applies.

"Calling the historically privileged names might, in fact, represent a kind of compensatory justice."

The little owl paced the whole length of the fence rail.

"On the other hand," he said, turning back to Gertrude, "when the historically privileged use offensive words toward the once-excluded, the words amount to an assault on their very selves. What's good for the goose is not necessarily good for the possum, if you see what I mean."

The Professor blinked his eyes and stepped back into the shade.

"That can't be right," replied Gertrude. "If hoof and paw and web and claw all walk on the same level ground, then the same rules apply to everyone. That's the constitution."

The Professor tut-tutted.

"Once again, the words of your constitution are a mask to hide your own privileged status. The constitution, after all, was written by farm animals. Its purpose was to uphold the binary division of animals into wild and tame; to privilege the ideology of tameness to the exclusion of other equally valid perspectives.

"In addition, the provision you just referred to promotes the illusion that all animals are the same. It blots out differences. It also fails to take into consideration historic injustices.

"Now, under Many-Animalism, we can reinterpret those words as an affirmation of difference. After all, though they might indeed walk on the same ground, the ground has never been level for all. And, indeed, paws and hooves cross the ground in quite different ways. Many-Animalism teaches us to respect the perspectives of others. That's what you're here to learn today.

"Now," said the owl, turning back to the rest of the class. "I want you all to make a list of words that you find offensive. At the end of this session, we'll make a list of all the things that no one must ever say."

CHAPTER 29

During their two weeks of Sensitivity Training, Gertrude learned to stop calling animals *wild* simply because they were born beyond the fence. Instead, they were to be called *forest-born*. Animals who sneaked across the fence were no longer *trespassers*, but *pre-citizens*, since eventually they'd all become voting members of society. Most of all, Gertrude learned not to be "insensitive," which meant saying anything that might upset the *forest-born* or to which a *pre-citizen* might possibly take offense. Anyone guilty of insensitivity could not take refuge in the constitution by claiming that it promised every animal a voice. The constitution didn't protect against the tongue's misuse. One insensitive word could lead to public humiliation and disgrace. Those convicted of insensitivity were now subject to various punishments, including expulsion from their "house" and a reduction in their daily rations.

After being pilloried throughout Orientation, Barlow proclaimed his guilt and apologized to the entire school. To make amends for his bad behavior, he said he and his mate would make room for more pre-citizens by not bringing any new pigs into the world this spring. Their sacrifice was immediately rewarded with a double helping from the morning bucket and the promise of extra fruit when the harvest came in.

In their two weeks under the owl's tutelage, the farm animals also learned that their system of government—and indeed their entire way of life—was an insult to nature and reason. Defending their former customs and habits was also considered offensive since it demonstrated a continued desire to dominate and exclude. Progressive opinion on the farm now held that the status quo was unacceptable. Radical changes were needed to make the farm more suitable to its rapidly growing population of forest-born citizens.

Kit, the Chief Executive, did all he could to accommodate the tide of newcomers with executive orders and special commissions, but they insisted that more sweeping changes were necessary to ensure justice and make them feel comfortable. Since the legislative process was slow and unpredictable—and many animals still resisted change—they bypassed the Animal Council and took their complaints directly to court. With a new forest-born occupant in the chair of Supreme Judge, they felt that route was the surest way to redress their grievances.

Once again, the Professor assumed the role of legal advocate for change. Speaking on behalf of the forest-born, he first succeeded in getting Chapel purged from the school's curriculum. He convinced the judge that its message of tameness was an unconstitutional infringement on the rights of pre-citizens. Those raised in the forest never had a direct relationship with man and so felt excluded by the language and symbols of spirit-shepherdhood. They should not be forced to listen to sermons about the benefits of tameness, but instead should be taught to celebrate their own breeds' special qualities and contributions to the farm. For this, he argued, they would need to study under teachers of their own species. *What could a duck teach a multi-talented beaver?* asked the Professor. Rather, the time had come to compel the native farm animals to study the forest-borns' unique abilities in required courses on Many-Animalism.

Likewise, the Winter Festival's crèche was deemed offensive, since the forest-born were excluded from its animal tableaux, and so it was banned from the barn and consigned permanently to the farmhouse basement. Animals wanting to celebrate Winter Festival by looking at the crèche and hearing sermons about tameness would henceforth have to meet privately in the basement.

The farm animals were saddened by the prospect of losing the crèche. But with Ike no longer around to deliver sermons, it wouldn't be the same anyway, they reasoned. They could accept having to creep up to the farmhouse to observe the miniature animals at prayer. They could still kneel before the manger and its heavenly messenger if they felt so inclined. What the farm animals objected to was the Professor's proposal to remove another religious symbol: the barn's NO TRESPASSING sign.

Privately, the cows, horses, and hens argued fiercely that they should keep the sign posted where it had always been, at the head of the farm's tablet of laws. They complained that the demands of the forest-born were simply outrageous. They swore that they'd never live to see that sign come down.

But when the time came to defend it before a large hostile crowd of forest-born animals, no one stepped forward to play advocate, fearing that they'd be subject to charges of insensitivity and legal recriminations. It was left to Eudora, the barn's oldest and most widely respected cow, to argue for keeping the sign.

"That sign was here before I was born," Eudora argued in low, reassuring tones. "It was put up by Grover himself, as a sign to all of us that the farm is not just a plot of ground enclosed by a fence, but a sacred place where we can all live together in peace and friendship. The sign says that there are domestic farm citizens who belong here and others who don't. It says to those dangerous predators who would destroy our way of life, 'KEEP OUT'—or face the consequences. Removing that sign would be a sacrilege. It would be a slap in the face to generations who gave their lives protecting Green Pastures Farm. It's more than just words or an abstract idea; it's a symbol. A symbol of who and what we are. No one has the right to take that sign down. That sign proclaims our first law. It's the bedrock and foundation of everything we believe."

When Eudora finished, the barn was silent as the night sky. The farm animals nodded and traded glances as if to confirm their own private thoughts.

Then the Professor stepped onto the floor and countered with words of his own.

"The question we should be asking," he said quietly, "is this: Is this farm going to be a place of inclusion or exclusion? Are we going to be an open, friendly, and welcoming society or perpetrators of xenophobia and hate?"

The little owl paced back and forth, challenging his viewers with large fathomless eyes.

"The constitution says, 'Many animals, one farm.' Are we going to follow our constitution and allow many animals onto this farm or be exclusive and keep them out?

"The constitution says, 'Every animal has a voice and an ear.' Are we going to silence the voices of the forest-born out of narrow-mindedness and fear or open our ears to their cries for equity and justice?

"The constitution itself requires that we take down that noxious sign, which has never spoken on behalf of justice, but instead is a symbol of hate. More than a bullet or arrow or butcher's knife, that sign is stab at the very heart of Many-Animalism. It is an offense against everything that walks or swims or flies on feathered wings. 'NO TRESPASSING.' Those are the words of the bully, the hunter, the overlord. Those words are an offense to everything sacred and decent on this good mother earth."

The barn owl paused to take a breath and to let his words sink in.

"Think how that sign must look to the hungry fawn or baby possum starving in the cropless woods," he said more quietly, in a voice now hoarse with emotion. "Leaving that sign up is nothing less than an act of murder. If it denies one starving weasel a small share in the bounty of Green Pastures Farm, we are all guilty of its death. We should take down that poisonous sign for shame, for very shame!"

The Professor surveyed the entire length and breadth of the assembly.

"I invite anyone who would starve that innocent child of the forest to stand up and affirm their belief in that sign right now. Go on, stand up if you believe in starving innocent babies to death. Stand up and defend that sign."

The owl stared into the heart of the crowd, waiting for someone, anyone, to come forward and meet his challenge. Finding no takers, he turned back to the judge.

"Very well then, Your Honor, I will accept your judgment on this matter, whatever it might be. Do the only thing you can now and reject this token of religious bigotry. It is clearly unconstitutional. I implore you on behalf of all the hungry and excluded of the world, tear down that miserable sign and set us free."

To no one's surprise, Rags wiped his teary eyes and ruled that the NO TRESPASSING sign had to come down immediately—not only from the barn's wall, but from everywhere it appeared on the farm. He further ruled that all of the signs were then to be collected and placed in a pile of dry kindling beneath the iron weather vane so that the first lightning strike might catch the pile on fire and purge the farm of its offensive message for all time.

After the judge concluded his ruling, the crowd bellowed and stamped approval, making the whole farm ring with their celebration.

Only Eudora looked up at the sign and sadly shook her head.

She cast a glance toward Shep, who was looking down at the floor with an expression of abject defeat.

As if sensing her stare, Shep looked up and met her eyes.

It was his turn now to take on the Professor. The next case threatened to turn the farm upside down. Though Eudora's shame and humiliation weighed on him heavily, Shep steeled himself to meet the challenge. For all of their sakes, he'd better get this one right.

CHAPTER 30

As the judge looked down on the assembly, Shep fidgeted with anxiety as he waited to present his argument. Beside him stood the Professor, cool and unflappable, waiting for the judge to hammer the crowd to silence.

At the first sound of the makeshift gavel, the owl leapt forward to state his case.

"Your Honor," the owl began, "in recent days, we have made some progress in achieving equity and fairness. Despite its history of exclusion, the farm has taken some small steps toward achieving a true Many-Animalist society. Though breedism remains a pervasive problem in our institutions, change is slowly coming as the new light of Many-Animalism illuminates the dark pockets of resistance that remain.

"And yet, despite these progressive developments," the Professor continued, "there is still one gross injustice that cries out for remedy. It is a law enacted when the farm was permeated by xenophobia. It is a law imposed by narrow-minded bigots upon the voiceless and powerless. A religious law enacted for the sole purpose of excluding those deemed unfit for domestic society.

"I am talking, of course, about the law that says animals on Green Pastures Farm must walk by day, not by night."

The owl stared intently at the judge, who, at the mention of the law, suddenly leaned forward with a look of rapt attention.

"What forest-born animal on this farm has not felt the pain and humiliation of being forced to violate a primary instinct of its nature?" asked the owl with a hunch of his wings.

"This unsound religious ordinance is not only the product of a dark, unenlightened era, but it is also clearly unconstitutional. It violates the constitution's second law that states that hoof, web, paw, and claw all walk on the same level ground.

"Now, how can the ground be level for all if half the breeds on this farm can barely see it through the oppressive glare of sunlight? How can animals claim to live on the same level ground if the law hurts the eye of some and forces their hearts and minds to labor according to awkward, unnatural rhythms?

"No," the Professor said, "this law is plainly unconstitutional. It must be overruled. Though the dog will argue to keep it, there is no reasonable argument for forcing every animal on this farm to walk by day. The second law of the constitution provides clear grounds for abolishing this unfair religious ordinance."

With that, the Professor shut his eyes, pulled his head down between his shoulders, and—as if to demonstrate the inarguable nature of his conclusion—appeared to go to sleep.

Startled by the owl's odd behavior, Shep stepped forward and awkwardly addressed the judge.

"In the forest," Shep began, with a sidelong glance at the owl, "small animals don't have the luxury of walking by day. They are surrounded by dangerous predators who would kill them and eat them on sight. And so to preserve their lives and give them a small measure of security, they creep about the forest by night under the cover of darkness.

"Generations of forest animals have lived in fear, their nights haunted by shadows of bears and wolves and their days haunted by dreams of pursuit and flight. Domesticity ended that primal nightmare. Farm animals now live safely behind fences, guarded by laws and protected by their large numbers, numbers which only a prosperous farm can support.

"We animals of Green Pastures Farm," Shep continued, "have generously allowed the forest-born to live here among us, protected by our laws and fences and guarded by our lives and blood. We allow them to share in our safety and security, to walk by day like free citizens instead of creeping about at night in fear of the large and powerful. Even the smallest chipmunk is safe here on the farm. He can walk boldly in the light of the sun unmolested by the mighty, the equal in every way of the largest bull or stallion.

"We must not be forced back into a skulking nocturnal existence to live in fear and privation. We have work to do on the farm. The difficult arts of planting and harvesting are best performed by day when we can see what we're doing and carefully measure our actions. The law 'Walk by Day, Not by Night' is not the product of bigotry and hate, but the fruit of long traditions carved out by generations of successful living. It would be wrong, no, suicidal, to cast it aside. Tameness requires light and farsighted vision. It withers like a plant when deprived of sunlight; it shrinks into the shadows where darkness and danger dwell."

Shep paused to take a breath and gauge the judge's reaction. So far, the raccoon looked respectful and attentive. Shep took a deep breath and launched into his conclusion.

"There is nothing in the constitution that requires us to abolish this long-standing and necessary law. We can walk on level ground under the steady sun far better than under the ever-changing moon and flickering stars. This law is fair, sensible, and constitutionally sound. Your Honor, you must uphold it for the well-being of the farm."

The farm animals responded to Shep's remarks with a hearty "Hear, hear" and loud stamping. To bring them to order, the judge had to pound his board with a tenpenny nail.

"I will need a minute to deliberate," the raccoon said when the crowd grew quiet. Then he retired behind a stack of bales to consider the arguments in private.

As they awaited the judge's return, the crowd quietly debated the issue among themselves. The general consensus was that Shep had won the case. Even the forest-born were certain the judge would rule in the dog's favor. They slumped a bit in anticipation of his ruling when the raccoon returned, mounted his hay bale, and hammered the room to order.

"It's true that nothing in the constitution specifically requires me to rule that the law 'Walk by Day' is unconstitutional," the judge began. "However, as the Professor pointed out, there are shadows and emanations in its language suggesting that to walk on level ground might require some adjustments to the law.

"In addition, there are cases when we must look beyond the written law to higher truths, times when we must look beyond this farm to the wider world and consider the practices and opinions of others.

"Now, in the widest perspective, Green Pastures Farm is a rather small place. Its domain can be measured in dozens or hundreds of acres. By contrast, the woods and mountains are large and boundless, beyond all measure. An animal can walk through the mountains and forests for days without crossing a border or coming upon a fence.

"Those vast domains are ruled by different laws than those enacted here by a few breeds of domesticated farm animals. The vast majority of the world's creatures live outside this farm. And when we consider how they live and by what laws and customs they regulate their activities, we see that most are in fact nocturnal, walking by night and sleeping by day.

"The founders of Green Pastures Farm were wise and farsighted animals. The constitution they created has many virtues. But above the laws they enacted is another, higher law. I'm speaking of natural law, whose extent spans the entire creation.

"Now every animal has a natural right to follow its own nature," said the judge. "There is no higher law than that. And natural law urges the majority of the forest's inhabitants—that is, the majority of animals in the world—to walk by night rather than by day."

The judge cleared his throat and assumed a grave expression.

"Therefore," he concluded somberly, "I rule that the law that says the animals of this farm must walk by day is unfair and unconstitutional. My own nature as a raccoon proclaims that a higher law abrogates the petty statutes enacted by a small group of self-serving farm animals.

"For too long this band has imposed its rules on nature's children. And so the time has come to restore things to their natural state."

A burst of cheers erupted from the forest-born as the farm animals dropped their heads and wept.

"From now on," continued the judge, "the law of Green Pastures Farm is not 'Walk by Day, Not by Night,' but the reverse. From now on we will walk by night and sleep by day, as nature demands. Those who violate the law are guilty of insensitivity and will be prosecuted and punished by starvation or expulsion."

The judge looked out and addressed the entire assembly.

"My fellow citizens," said Rags. "There are still several hours of sunlight. Go find yourself a place to sleep. The new workday will begin at sunset. Students and workers must be at their stations by dark."

CHAPTER 31

"We made him judge, not king," protested Raymond. "In one day how can he declare practically every law we ever had unconstitutional?"

The rooster kicked the dust and glared at Shep and Eudora.

"You dogs and cows can adapt to working at night, but for us ducks and chickens, this is a nightmare. When it's dark, birds go to roost. The hens are beside themselves. As for me, how am I supposed to stop crowing? I've been crowing every dawn almost since the day I hatched."

The poor rooster looked exhausted from rising at dusk, observed Shep. When the judge said that most of the world's animals walked by night, he'd left birds out of the equation.

"That's not all," Raymond said. "There are big problems in the chicken coop. I don't know how much longer I can keep things under control. In the last few days, several chicks have gone missing. Duke found some feathers in the grass behind the barn. The raccoons blame hawks, but if you ask me, they've been looking a little plumper lately. And of course, your own stomachs tell you what's been happening to the eggs."

"You don't need to tell me that," replied Jessy. "Pip's almost sick with hunger. I can hardly stomach the swill Gert's been sending us.

It's all oats and corn—hardly a drop of egg or milk. The possums must be drinking it by the bucket."

"It's going to get worse," Raymond said glumly. "I might as well tell you, the quails have convinced the hens to withhold their eggs. They say the dogs and pigs have no right to *appropriate* the product of hens. That's the word of the day over there: *appropriate*. I've tried to explain, those are *unfertilized* eggs that get gathered in the morning. But the hens are vowing to hold them back to show solidarity with the quails."

Mara, the big gray and white mare, shook her head and pawed at the barnyard dirt. "There's a section of fence down in the cattle pasture," she said softly. "It looks like the rails have been chewed through by a beaver. With Garth out there, I don't think there's any immediate danger, but it's not good. Once the wild ones—er, the forest-born—sense weakness, they're bound to start probing our defenses."

The big mare shook her mane and nervously twitched her tail.

"I don't know what's gotten into Kit," she added quietly. "It's just the same with Garth. They think that because they're big and strong, there's no danger. The sheep and ducks know better. What endangers one of us endangers the whole farm. But until giant bears come strolling across the pasture with blood in their eyes, the two of them will think nothing's changed."

"Well, at least some of the crops will soon be coming in," said Raymond. "I just went by the garden and the vegetables almost look ripe."

Not even Raymond was truly cheered by the prospect of fresh vegetables. But the little group of friends pretended to be glad that there would soon be food for the farm's growing population. As they separated to return to homes and families, they declared their undying loyalty to the farm and vowed to maintain vigilance in the face of whatever changes future rulings might bring.

A few days later, another case had the whole farm buzzing. At the request of a group of possums, the judge ruled that the old farmhouse that had stood empty since the death of Grover would provide a residence for the forest-born. The possums and raccoons would live on the second floor and the groundhogs, chipmunks, and beavers on the first. The new residence would also serve as the sixth house in the farm's political scheme, the judge ruled, with its own representative on the Animal Council.

Shep argued against providing the forest-born with their own special residence. They were already well-integrated into the other houses, he argued, and so didn't need a place of their own. Furthermore, they were represented by the other houses and didn't need a seat reserved on the Council just for them.

The Judge, however, felt differently. He declared that the forest-born were an excluded minority and so needed a "safe place" away from the others where they could feel at home.

"Besides," added the judge, "in a Many-Animalist society, the forest-born should be free to celebrate their own unique values and identities. On Green Pastures Farm, we celebrate biodiversity. Having a house for our new citizens shows that we value their presence here."

Using his opponents' favorite tactic, Shep declared that it would be *breedist* and xenophobic to allow only forest-born animals into the old farmhouse. In fairness, the new house should be open to all.

To counter this objection, the Professor stepped in to clarify the judge's legal reasoning.

"The term *breedism*," explained the barn owl, "cannot be applied in this situation. By definition, breedism can only be practiced by the historically powerful against the weak and excluded. In this case, it is the historically excluded who will be setting themselves apart, in order to resist institutional oppression."

"So," Shep countered, thinking to expose the owl's faulty logic, "the chickens have to let the possums into the henhouse, but the possums don't have to let the chickens into theirs?"

"Precisely," replied the Professor. "The chickens once excluded possums from the farm; possums have never excluded chickens from the forest. If you were a forest-born animal, you would instinctively understand this."

"But why should they have their own house," asked Shep, "and their own representative when they already have votes in the others? The possums control what used to be called the pigpen. And they have their own caucuses in the other houses, too, so their voices are already heard. Why do they need their own seat reserved for them?"

The Professor smiled wryly.

"I suppose your next question will be, why can't the dogs and horses form their own caucuses to represent their special needs? As if those powerful animals ever lacked a voice on this farm. No, I won't let you hide your power-play behind a mask of fairness and objectivity. The judge has already ruled. The forest-born will now enjoy a privilege formerly enjoyed only by chickens and cattle and pigs.

"I'm sorry, my friend," the owl chuckled. "You'll just have to get used to living in a society based on equality and social justice."

In the following days, with the memory of the latest judicial ruling still fresh in mind, Raymond went about his business in a constant state of anxiety. Several times now Shep had argued his case brilliantly, and yet the farm animals had lost every important decision. It was pretty obvious that power had gone to the raccoon's head. He wasn't even trying to interpret the law anymore. After all, thought Raymond, Rags was a raccoon himself, so how much objectivity and fairness could be expected from him?

With a mirthless chuckle the rooster recalled how the farm's troubles had begun by trying to be fair to Xena, the wounded deer. Now the animals they'd welcomed onto the farm were accusing them of injustice while excluding them.

To top things off, as soon as they got settled in the farmhouse, the raccoons formed an organization called "The Breed." The group had begun in a "Raccoon Studies" class in school. Now claiming they couldn't get justice from the Animal Council, they marched about the farm nearly every day shouting about xenophobia and demonstrating against whatever they didn't like.

To match them, the possums soon formed an underground society of their own called the "Marsupial Militia." Working in the shadows, the group avoided public demonstrations, using whispered threats and hints of violence to get their way.

Recently, they'd sent word through the grapevine that Raymond had better stop crowing every morning or he'd face retaliation.

In response to their whisper campaign, Raymond had stood firm. Stating that he worked by night and slept by day as the law demanded, he proclaimed that he would crow in the morning if he liked—or at any other time that he felt like it.

Today, with all their legal setbacks fresh in mind, the rooster was in no mood to be trifled with. When he walked into the chicken yard and saw a young possum behaving suspiciously, he acted without hesitation.

"What are you doing there?" he demanded, then reached toward the possum's shoulder with his beak.

Instead of answering, the possum tried to duck under the building and escape.

Finding he didn't fit, he turned and made a mad dash for the henhouse door.

Raymond raced after him, sputtering with rage.

"Halt!" he shouted, flexing his spurs as he ran.

When the fugitive turned into the doorway, Raymond spied a pair of scaly legs dangling from the possum's mouth. The little thief had been eating a dead chick when Raymond interrupted him

Stifling an impulse to vomit, Raymond followed the possum through the henhouse door. He stopped just over the threshold to let his eyes adjust to the darkness.

Across the floor, he spied a shadow slowly moving toward him through the gloom.

No, not one shadow, but two or three. They were gliding across the floor, fanning out as they approached.

Raymond couldn't make out who or what they were, so he took a few steps forward, turned his head, and squinted into the darkness.

Suddenly, from behind, he felt hot breath on his neck.

"Let's hear you crow now, your lordship," hissed a familiar voice in his ear.

Startled, Raymond turned and saw several more large shadows advancing from his rear.

In an instant, they were upon him.

Suddenly, an iron vise clamped the rooster's windpipe. Lightning bolts of pain shot down the length of his neck.

A large possum had fastened his jaws on Raymond's throat. As needle teeth pierced his flesh and windpipe, Raymond flapped his wings and tried to leap away. But a second mouth seized him from behind and held him fast.

"Bite harder," the first voice hissed—the last thing Raymond heard before blacking out.

A minute later his headless body was running across the henhouse floor bumping into walls and stumbling over the corpses of dead hens.

"Pick the head up," a voice hissed, "and put it on the fence post outside where he crows. I want everyone to see it there."

A possum bent over and picked up the rooster's head by its comb and held it up for the others to see.

After a soft chuckle, he hid the head in his fur and casually strolled outside.

"We'll leave the henhouse one at a time," said the leader.

"Later, after washing off, we'll all take separate paths back to the pen."

CHAPTER 32

The news of Raymond's beheading and the slaughter of several hens sent shock waves across the farm. The horses declared they would trample to death whoever murdered their dear brave friend the rooster. The dogs immediately set about tracking down his killer.

After investigating the murder scene, the dogs concluded that the killer was most likely a possum, because the only scent they could detect on the body and its immediate surroundings was possum scent.

The problem was that everything in and around the henhouse smelled of possum since almost as many possums lived there as hens.

Duke, who had the best nose on the farm, led the investigation. After tracing the scent from the fence post to the water trough to the pigpen, he declared that the only smell he could clearly identify belonged to Oscar, who lived in the pen and who'd been seen earlier that day in the chicken coop.

Oscar, however, vociferously denied any involvement in Raymond's death, saying he worked in the chicken coop at night collecting eggs, and so naturally his smell was found on everything.

Since Duke was the only witness capable of identifying him, the judge wouldn't allow the case against Oscar to proceed, so the possum was released pending the discovery of further evidence.

In the meantime, every bird on the farm was paralyzed by terror. Pierre tried to calm them down by urging them to reflect on the motives behind Raymond's murder.

"The question we must ask ourselves is, 'What have we done to bring this on ourselves?'" the duck declared. "Until we know why they hate us, we can't begin to understand this awful event.

"Did our pride and arrogance set us up for this catastrophe? Perhaps we should set up a commission to investigate the root causes of this terrible tragedy."

When Gertrude spied her own goslings nodding agreement, she stepped forward and rebuked the duck.

"What are you talking about, Pierre? The problem isn't us. It's murderous possums."

"Silence! Are you mad?" the duck hissed, looking wildly about. "Do you want your insane charge to be heard?"

"Pierre is right," whispered Hetty. "It's no longer safe to talk. The walls have ears."

"The Marsupial Militia has threatened retaliation against anyone who blames possums for the tragedy," added a nervous little hen. "Anyway, it's not fair to blame all of them for the actions of one or two."

The goslings nodded agreement. "Kit said that possums are by nature peaceful," observed one, setting the others to nodding again.

"He's asked Olive and Oliver to advise him on how to increase understanding between possums and farm animals," added another of Gertrude's daughters.

"As he well should," said Pierre. "We must appease the possums any way we can. A quick survey of the farm makes the situation clear. We chickens, ducks, and geese are barely maintaining our numbers. The possums, on the other hand, are proliferating like grass. In a year or two this farm will belong to them. We birds and cattle and dogs will be a fading minority. We must learn to accommodate the forest-born or find ourselves extinct."

"We only have ourselves to thank for that," muttered Gertrude.

"Ourselves?" clucked Hetty. "Ourselves? It isn't chickens stealing eggs and killing chicks. Oh, what am I saying? I'd better shut my mouth before someone takes *my* head."

"We have to bring this before the Animal Council," insisted Gertrude. "It's no use going to the judge. We won't get justice there."

"The Council," sniffed a hen. "Three of the six houses have already gone over to the forest-born. We're deadlocked. Besides, any motion we pass will only be declared unconstitutional. Whoever thought it was a good idea to appoint Rags to be judge?"

"We should go to the cows and horses," said Hetty. "We should tell them to drive the trespass—uh, the forest-born—off the farm, every last one!"

After saying her piece, the hen almost collapsed in a state of nervous exhaustion.

"That's vigilantism," sniffed Pierre. "We are civilized farm animals. We must rely on the law. If only we knew what the wil . . . er, the forest-born . . . wanted, we could surely find some way to satisfy them."

"I'm keeping my mouth shut," said a goose. "Raymond was a brave and mighty rooster. After what happened to him, I'm not risking my neck to say a word around here. Let the horses and dogs fix things. They're big and well-armed. This isn't the time for us birds to risk our necks."

While the geese and chickens discussed what course to take, the dogs redoubled their efforts to catch Raymond's killer. Each evening before dusk, Shep slipped out before the other animals awoke, to investigate suspicious activity. The first thing he discovered was a set of fresh hoofprints that led from the ruined fence to the cornfield.

Pig prints, his nose indicated. And not an ordinary domestic pig, either, but the deep pungent prints of a large tusk-wielding boar.

So far the boar had been satisfied with eating his fill of corn and sneaking back through the broken fence. But once he got used to trotting about the farm gorging himself on their crops, there's no telling what he might do. A wild boar was too much for Shep to handle alone. It would take all the dogs, working together with other large animals, to deal with such a formidable adversary.

While considering how best to handle the boar, Shep galloped toward the orchards to check on the ripening fruit.

But before he got there, he could see something was terribly wrong in the nearby vegetable garden.

Half of the crop was trampled flat, and the rest had been ravaged by hungry marauders. Half-eaten squash, cucumbers, and pumpkins were scattered everywhere.

Shep sniffed the scattered rinds and pulpy footprints from one end of the garden to the other, but his nose told him what his heart already knew. The only smell was the oily scent of groundhog. They'd had one wild orgy of a feast.

Shep didn't want to repeat their failure with Raymond's killer, so this time he wanted the other dogs to identify the scent too. He ran to the barn and summoned his mate Jessy. When they returned to the garden, Jessy confirmed his analysis. The only scent there was of groundhog. Both of them could witness to that fact.

The sun had barely set on the farm when the two border collies were in the barn testifying to the judge.

"So," said the judge, still wiping the sleep from his eyes. "You both attest to the fact that the only scent in the garden belongs to ground-hogs? If there are no objections, then, I'd like to order that . . ."

"I have an objection, Your Honor," proclaimed a soft voice from above.

The Professor fluttered down and stood before the court, looking up at the bleary-eyed raccoon.

"Before we act hastily, I would like to ask the witness a question or two, if I may."

The dozen or so spectators, all sleepy-eyed barn residents, shuffled their feet with impatience. A raid on the garden was a matter of the utmost urgency. Action had to be taken at once.

The judge nodded at Jessy. "Please respond to the Professor's questions," he advised. Then he nodded at the owl to get things moving along.

"So," said the owl, eyeing the witness narrowly, "you stated that the only identifiable scent was that of groundhogs, isn't that right?"

"Yes," replied Jessy.

"There were no other scents there? None but the groundhogs?"

The owl stared at the border collie as if to spur her faulty memory.

"No, only theirs," the dog said unsurely.

An awkward smile dawned on Jessy's face.

"Well, and, of course there was also Shep's," she stammered. "He'd, ah, been all over the garden, smelling everything."

"Ahhhhhhh," said the Professor with a crafty smile.

He turned back to the judge with an air of supreme confidence.

"Your Honor, the evidence has been tainted. It is unfair to charge the groundhogs with unlawful invasion of the garden when in fact the evidence might lead us just as surely to another conclusion."

The owl glanced across the barn at Shep.

"I don't mean to impugn our well-meaning friend," the owl added quickly. "But with the only witnesses being Shep and his loyal mate, I don't think we can proceed with this accusation. This charge might very well be the fruit of stereotyping by an overzealous dog—one known to be hostile to pre-citizens and the newly enfranchised."

"Your Honor," interjected Shep. "I was only there to investigate, as everyone knows. This is not like the other case where only Duke could identify the killer. Jessy confirms my testimony. The only scent in the garden is groundhogs—"

Before Shep could finish, a large angry groundhog stepped up to admonish the judge.

"This is outrageous," he said. "What else would the garden smell of but groundhogs, eh? We've been raising those vegetables with no help from anyone—much less a lazy dog. We know why the garden smells of us. What's the only other scent there, eh? None but this dog's. You draw your own conclusions, Your Honor. It looks to me like a certain border collie has been profiling again—or someone's trying to cover up his own involvement in the crime."

"With all due respect, Your Honor," said Shep. "We're missing the main point here. The point is the garden has been ravaged. Food that belongs to everyone was stolen by a few. Somebody has to be held accountable. In the meantime, I'd like to protect the evidence. Please let me to go back to make sure no one enters the garden. Duke has the best nose on the farm. I'm sure once he checks, he'll confirm my testimony."

The judge paused to consider Shep's request.

"All right," he said finally. "We'll call in Duke and have him smell the garden. But you're not the one to stand guard tonight. Your scent being there already makes you a suspect. I'll appoint some guards to stand watch till tomorrow night, when we'll meet here again to reassess the situation. Till then, stay away from the garden. That goes for everyone here."

CHAPTER 33

Moments after the court-appointed guards arrived, a crowd of angry groundhogs gathered beside the vegetable garden to demand that Shep apologize. The groundhogs were soon joined by other demonstrators from the farmhouse. Taking up positions along the garden's border, the Marsupial Militia stood in a tight line with arms crossed, defying anyone to break through their ranks and enter the forbidden garden. The raccoons of The Breed roamed about chanting, "Stop profiling!! Stop profiling!" while glaring at spectators who'd come to see the damage for themselves.

The guards—three frightened ewes and a young raccoon—stood helplessly by as the groundhogs threw ruined vegetables at the dogs, who stood a short distance off, waiting for the judge. By the time the judge and Duke approached, the situation threatened to turn violent.

Then suddenly amidst the noise and confusion, a pack of raccoons marched up to the garden and parted ranks, allowing two skunks to dart from among them into the garden.

The guards watched in stunned surprise as cries rang out and the spectators fled the scene. The air reeked with the odor of skunk. No one wanted to risk getting sprayed. And so, undeterred by the guards, the skunks frisked about the ruined garden, spreading their smell over every leaf, stalk, and rind.

By the time the judge arrived, the scene was so contaminated that an examination was impossible. Clutching his nose, the judge galloped away on the heels of Duke, whose eyes were weeping from the smell. The big Lab ran blindly toward the barn, baying and howling as he went.

For days afterward, both sides debated whether the groundhogs or Shep was guilty of destroying the garden. Since it was no longer possible to prove either case, the debate grew rancorous. But the destruction of the garden was soon eclipsed by trouble from a different quarter.

The forest animals beyond the fence were confused at first by the farm's shift to a nocturnal schedule, but once they realized that the animals now worked by night, they altered their own habits and ventured more boldly onto the farm under cover of darkness in search of food or prey. Instead of huddling all night in the safety of barns and shelters, the farm animals now walked through the dark alone or in small groups as they went about their daily chores, leaving them open to attack. Foxes and ferrets hid in the dark orchards, snatching pickers that strayed too far from the work gangs.

After several pickers were found slaughtered, the possums and raccoons refused to come down from the trees. Instead, they stayed in the branches, stuffing themselves with fruit till their bellies were nearly bursting.

The horses and pigs were left to work in their former fashion. The horses plucked what they could from the low branches while the pigs followed, scavenging scraps from the ground. The animals who couldn't reach fruit went without it. Stacks of empty baskets leaned crookedly against the walls of the storage sheds, unfilled. No one worked for the common good by drying fruit for the coming winter.

By day, while the animals slept, their fences were assaulted by troops of marauding beavers. Calling themselves "Earth's Avengers," they leveled whole sections of fence, cutting not only the rails but gnawing the posts off at the ground.

Now that the farm's borders were no longer patrolled by dogs, each species of farm animal was left to guard its home alone. In the cattle pasture, Garth, the bull, watched over his gently rolling meadows. Kit and the mares watched over their fields as they grazed and galloped about. But the sheep, who occupied the farm's furthermost outpost, felt exposed and unsafe. Convinced that coyotes and lions lurked just beyond their pasture, they went to the Animal Council and demanded help.

"The time has come for our resident beavers to march out there and fix those fences," Emma demanded. "It's outrageous to leave them in such disrepair. It was my understanding that this's why beavers were allowed on the farm in the first place."

A murmur of assent arose from the sheep delegation.

"What do you need fences for?" asked a beaver sulkily. "There's nothing to fear but yourselves."

"What's that supposed to mean?" demanded Emma.

"I mean," replied the beaver, "why should we go out there and sweat all night putting up fences just because you sheep are afraid of the dark? You're a bunch of scaredy cats."

"I wouldn't be afraid of the dark if there weren't wild beavers out there chewing up fences."

"How do you know it's beavers cutting them down?" demanded Tooth, stepping forward to join his friend. "You sheep are profiling again. Why don't you just admit that you hate beavers?"

"What else could cut those rails?" retorted Emma. "It's not wild ducks nibbling those posts to the ground."

Little Rags stepped forward and waved a fist in the air.

"This is the sort of breedism we've had to live with since the day my folks were lured onto this farm. Now that you lazy farm animals aren't getting waited on paw and hoof, you want to send us back to the forest. For all we know, you tore those fences down yourselves to stigmatize us. Instead of blaming us for your problems, why don't you confront your own xenaphobia?"

His fellow raccoons took up their leader's chant.

"Xenaphobia! Xenaphobia! Xenaphobia!" they shouted with pumping fists.

At the charge of xenophobia, the sheep suddenly looked abashed. Only Emma had the presence of mind to shout above the raccoons' protest.

"It isn't xenaphobia lurking out there in the forest. If you don't like it here on Green Pastures, why don't you and your friends go join your wild cousins out there?"

The ewe's remark sparked another round of shouts and angry accusations. Soon the beavers and raccoons threatened to disrupt the meeting.

The crowd was finally called back to their senses by the ringing of a large cowbell. The Professor hammered the rusty relic with his beak so hard he almost knocked it off its hook.

"There, there, there," he said as the crowd began to settle. "There's no need for hysteria. Let's settle this like reasonable animals. Remember our traditions. We're not here to bay and howl, but to make intelligent decisions after engaging in well-reasoned debate."

Suddenly, Eudora sidled up beside the little barn owl.

"The Professor's right," she said. "This is not our way."

"Emma," she said, turning to the agitated ewe, "please tell the Council, calmly, just exactly what it is you want."

The old ewe raised her head and stepped up to the Council.

"We want just what I said. To get those fences fixed. And if necessary, to teach those buck-toothed vandals a lesson if they don't stop tearing them down."

"We're not fixing 'em," muttered Tooth. "Those beavers are my friends and kin. You call them buck-toothed vandals again and you'll be sorry."

"Now, now," tut-tutted the Professor. "Let's be reasonable here."

He turned to Emma.

"Precisely *why* should we re-erect those broken fences?" he asked softly. "A more pertinent question might be, why have fences at all?"

The old ewe widened her eyes in disbelief.

"Why, to keep out unwanted guests, why else have fences?" she said.

"But isn't that *exclusive*?" asked the Professor. "You don't want to be exclusive, do you?"

Every eye was now fixed on the nervous ewe.

"Well, no, not exclusive," she stammered. "Just, you know, to include the kind of animals we want; the well-behaved ones."

"Ah. The kind of animals we want," repeated the owl slyly.

Disgruntled catcalls rippled through the crowd.

"That is to say," said the owl. "There are certain breeds of animals that belong on the farm and others that don't?"

"I didn't say breeds," protested Emma. "We already have beavers here. What I meant was—"

"What you meant," shouted Little Rags," is that you're a breedist ewe! You called us 'wild' a minute ago. Everyone heard you. You know the penalty for that. Starvation or exile.

"Mr. Chief Executive," he said, turning now to Kit, "we can't have that kind of talk in a Many-Animalist society like ours. Enforce the law. Deport this xenaphobic ewe right now. If you don't, we're going to rattle this barn to its foundation. No justice, no peace on the farm."

"But you said we were supposed to debate the issue," protested Emma, growing frantic at the prospect of punishment. "I was only speaking on behalf of my house."

"I'm sorry," Kit said, addressing Emma. "The law's the law. We'll discuss your situation in a moment."

"But what about the fences?" piped up a voice from the flock of indignant sheep.

"There's no place in a Many-Animalist society for fences," said the Professor sternly. "Their only purpose is to exclude. Do we want to live in a world divided into herds and factions, or do we want to live in a world without borders and divisions?

"No," he said, "with the exception of crows, which are filthy uncivilized beings lacking all morality and fellow-feeling, this farm should be open to any who want to come. There are no reasonable grounds to exclude any living creature from Green Pastures Farm. Those who object are motivated solely by xenophobia. And xeno-phobia must be stamped out on this farm."

CHAPTER 34

After sulking all day in the barn, Pip sneaked out at dusk before his parents awoke. Then, with a confident swagger that belied his nervousness, he walked up to the farmhouse's back door.

Two burly raccoons stood blocking the little swinging flap that served as the rear entrance.

"What are you doing up here, butt-sniffer?" asked the guard on Pip's right. "No dogs allowed. This house is for the forest-born."

"I want to talk to Little Rags," said Pip. "He's my friend. I want to come in."

The raccoons laughed derisively.

"I'll bet you do," said the guard. "What's the matter, pooch, you hungry?"

The two guards tittered and snorted through their noses.

"What does it matter to you?" asked Pip, whose stomach was indeed aching. All he'd eaten for days was a mush made of corn and oats soaked in well water. The gruel was hard to swallow and left him feeling empty and unsatisfied all day. A more pleasing odor wafted from the windows on the second floor.

"I'm not here looking for food. But somebody's eating eggs up there," he said.

Puffing out his chest to make himself look bigger, he added, "Why don't you two just step aside and let me pass?"

"Eating eggs?" asked the guard. "You must be hallucinating, dog. I don't see no eggs around here."

"What are you doing here?" asked the second guard, eyeing Pip suspiciously. "You think 'cause you're a dog we have to let you in? Ha! Your day's over, Rover. Take a walk—before I call my friends."

"Look," replied Pip, "I'm not here to eat your eggs." He lowered his voice. "I'm here because I want to join you."

The guard twitched his whiskers. "What are you talking about?" he sniffed. "You're a dog. What is it exactly that you want to join?"

Pip stepped closer and whispered, "I want to join The Breed."

The two raccoons laughed so hard they doubled over. Finally, after catching their breath, they straightened up and regarded Pip more soberly.

"Only raccoons can join," they said. "Now get off the porch, pooch, and drag your sorry tail back down to your cow friends at the barn. No dogs allowed."

Stung by the rebuff, Pip marched back toward the barnyard, fuming over his mistreatment by the raccoons. He should have torn into them for their snide remarks, he thought bitterly. That would give them something to laugh about.

The raccoons were right about one thing, though. A barn full of old milk cows was no place for a young dog. He should be out herding sheep—or chasing rabbits. His uncle Duke talked fondly of chasing rabbits—back in the old days before it became a crime.

Pip turned from the barnyard and ambled to the rear of the barn, where he sat down in a patch of standing weeds to sulk.

He sniffed the dirt and scratched his ear, digging at fleas. He might as well hide here for a while, he thought, to avoid starting work.

The sound of muffled footsteps startled him from his reverie.

"What's the matter, kid?" asked a low nasal voice. "They wouldn't let you into their little clubhouse?"

Suddenly Pip's nostrils burned with a strange pungent smell. He turned to confront his visitor and met the long sharp snout and keen eyes of a fox.

"What are you doing here?" Pip asked, tensing for trouble. He was taller and sturdier, but the fox looked swift and cunning—and poised as if to spring. The stink he gave off was almost overpowering.

"Why?" asked the fox. "You going to run me off?" He chuckled softly. "It looks to me like you might need a friend."

Pip eyed the fox closely, startled by the keenness of his observation. The truth was, Pip did need a friend. Young Bronson had lately abandoned him to spend all his time cavorting about the farm with a wild boar, who'd taken him under his wing. Without Bronson, Pip had not one soul to confide in on the farm.

"Maybe," Pip ventured. "But you didn't answer my question. What are you doing here?"

"Are you a sentry?" the fox asked. "I thought you folks had given up patrolling borders. That's the word out in the forest. Or are you the last line of defense?"

"Very funny," said Pip. "You got a name?"

"If necessary," replied the fox. "You can call me Solomon."

"Odd name," said Pip. "What's it mean?"

"It means 'peace.'"

The fox grinned slyly.

"Well, Mr. Peace, have you been spying on me? How'd you know I couldn't get into the farmhouse?"

The fox edged a bit closer.

"If you still want to go," he whispered, "I can arrange it."

Pip perked his ears. "You serious?"

Solomon looked toward the western sky.

"It's almost dark," he said, squinting. "I can get you in tonight. It's a special holiday."

"What about the guards?" asked Pip.

The fox chuckled. "Come on," he said, and galloped off in the direction of the farmhouse. Pip hesitated a moment, then set off after the fox, who glanced back over his shoulder to urge him on. Pip quickly overtook Solomon, and within seconds they were at the farmhouse door.

At the sight of the fox, the two raccoons stiffened.

"He can't go in," they said with a glance toward Pip.

"He's with me," said the fox and advanced toward the door.

The guards exchanged nervous glances.

"Uh, he's a dog," said the guard, edging back and eyeing Pip nervously.

The fox smiled. "That's not a dog," he said with a friendly nudge of Pip's shoulder.

"You're looking at the newest member of the Canine Brotherhood."

CHAPTER 35

Pip was shocked by what he saw inside the farmhouse. As they passed through the building, the first thing he noticed was that every room was occupied by a different species—the kitchen by chipmunks, the dining room by squirrels, and the living room by groundhogs—all busily going about their business. Pip and Solomon were the only outsiders in every room through which they passed. The other animals regarded them suspiciously, but stood back, displaying an awkward deference—as if they were visiting dignitaries too exalted to approach.

Pip smiled to himself, realizing it was because they were large canines. Their gleaming teeth and cunning wits commanded respect.

They didn't visit the basement, but Pip's nose told him what lived down there. The odor of skunk rose through the floorboards, permeating the house like gas. The skunks didn't have to post guards at the cellar door. The smell alone would choke visitors to death.

The second thing that struck Pip about the farmhouse was that each room was ruled over by the breed's largest male. The females kept out of sight, gossiping among themselves in the corners or quietly nursing their young—except when they were waiting on the males. The idea that all animals walked on the same level ground seemed utterly alien here.

Pip spotted a large groundhog in a chair being served by a pair of sleek young females half his size.

"How'd all the big males get voted into office?" he whispered to Solomon.

The fox stopped in his tracks and stared at Pip.

"Voted?" he asked. "What a quaint idea."

He pointed his muzzle at a series of large symbols etched on the adjacent wall.

After a moment's study, Pip unraveled their meaning.

Fang and Claw
Over Hoof and Paw.

As comprehension dawned, a smile bloomed on Pip's countenance.

Solomon grinned. "Stick with me, kid, and you'll go places. Tonight you're in for the time of your life."

Upstairs, they passed through the possums' and raccoons' quarters, then through a hallway that led to a large dark room with shuttered windows. Once inside, Pip was surprised to see two more foxes and a large coyote across the room.

"What's that coyote doing here?" he whispered to Solomon—and immediately regretted his mistake.

The two foxes glared at Solomon. At the sight of the strange dog, the coyote edged backward.

Then observing Pip's youth and size, he grinned, displaying large yellow teeth.

"So you have a little apprentice," said the coyote with a hoarse laugh. He sniffed Pip's scent on the air without approaching.

"Forgive me," he said, sidling forward. "For a moment, I thought you were that blasted cur named Shep."

Pip decided not to mention his kinship with the blasted cur. The coyote looked large and ill-tempered. There was no point in alienating him.

Solomon cleared his throat and introduced Pip.

"Cy, this is my friend Pip," he said with an air of pride. "He wants to be initiated."

He turned to Pip.

"Pip, this is Cy. You'd better take a good look because he's a quite the trickster. Tonight he's going to introduce you to the Mysteries."

Pip didn't know what he meant by "the Mysteries" and he wasn't about to ask. Instead, he stood up tall and looked Cy straight in the eye.

"When do I get initiated?" he asked.

The coyote smiled. "In due time.

"But first," he added with a quick glance over his shoulder, "we have the night to celebrate. Forgive me if I don't accompany you downstairs. I have to get ready for my sermon."

Pip cast a doubtful glance toward Solomon. The coyote seemed the last creature on earth to deliver a sermon. At first, Pip thought he was joking, but the others took the remark seriously.

"We'd better get downstairs and gather the minions then," said Solomon to the other foxes.

After Cy slipped into the dark hallway, his two lieutenants relaxed and stood at ease.

The larger one stepped closer and gave Pip a toothy smile. "Welcome to Wilderness House," he said.

Turning back to Solomon, he added with a grin, "I hate to say it, but the little fellow doesn't look much like a wilding. And they say you're such a sterling judge of character."

Solomon winked reassuringly at Pip.

"Oh, don't you worry about young Pip here. He's a wild one, all right. Just give him time. He'll surprise you, this one."

The two sentinels eyed Pip silently, taking his measure.

Then, as the two guards consulted in whispers, Pip hissed to Solomon, "We're not supposed to say *wild*. It's offensive."

Overhearing, the foxes burst out laughing.

"No, *you're* not supposed to say *wild*," said one, setting off another round of laughter.

"That's right," said his companion. "After tonight, you'll see the word in a different light."

By the time Pip and Solomon joined the others downstairs, the three main rooms were packed with spectators. A stage had been fashioned from the dining room table for the coyote's sermon—if that's what it would be. Pip remained skeptical. The only sermon he'd ever heard had been delivered by Ike, who looked the part of a prophet, with his depthless yellow eyes and snowy beard. The coyote was far more laconic and had a shifty look about the eyes.

Like the windows upstairs, the ones down here were shuttered, leaving the rooms in near darkness. The only illumination entered through a little porthole window that glowed with the sun's last light.

Close-packed and growing restive, the possums, raccoons, and groundhogs waited for the speaker to appear.

Suddenly, a cloud seemed to pass over the window, plunging the room into darkness.

The crowd sucked in its breath, then let out a collective sigh.

Pip's eyes took longer to adjust than the others as he stared through the gloom. Then a dim glow returned to the window, casting a dull light across the floor.

Pip blinked his eyes in wonder. The coyote was now standing on the tabletop, staring down at him with an ironic toothy leer.

Pip hadn't heard so much as a claw click as Cy entered.

To prevent being fooled again, he pricked his ears.

Now he could hear the faint rasp of the coyote's breath as he gathered a lungful of air and stood up tall to speak.

CHAPTER 36

"Once the world was round and whole as an egg," said the coyote. "Forest and ocean covered the earth like a warm shell. The birds of the air, the fish of the sea, and the animals that walked the ground lived each unto itself alone, in harmony with the world's wholeness. The sheep knew not of the herd, the birds knew not of the flock, and the fish knew not of the school, but each walked or flew or swam by itself alone, living in communion with the All that is. Time was not, as all things lived in the Now, knowing neither before nor after. All creatures walked in the sun, which shone on everything, giving life and warmth to all.

"Then one day Man was born, the runt of earth's litter. Naked and clawless, he stole the day for himself, banishing his fellow creatures to night and chaos.

"But still the man hungered inside for more. Not content with all that is, he fashioned tools, and used them to tear the earth's flesh into furrows. He stole a spark from the sun and named it fire and held it against night's darkness like a shield. He chopped off limbs of trees to steal their heat. He killed animals and roasted their flesh to steal their life for himself.

"But being incomplete, the man still felt a hunger he could not satisfy. Walking unsteadily on two legs, he envied the sturdy creatures who walked on four. Living in groups, he envied the solitary ones who lived by strength alone. He hated himself for being but half-made and craved the company of those who were made whole. So in his incompleteness, he lured the creatures of the night to his fires and subdued them with cunning tricks.

"With magic of his human will, he transformed a wolf pup to a dog, thus giving birth to the slavish breed of curs that live on his scraps and refuse. With the help of his new servant, the man drove the wild creatures into flocks and herds so that they might be more easily taken. Then with his cunning tools, the man cut down trees and fashioned their wood to make fences. He encircled the open fields to pen his herds, and he called these prisons 'pastures.'

"With the help of the dog, man corralled the mighty stallion. Then he lulled the horse's will with words and broke his spirit with strong ropes. He bestrode that mighty thunderer so that he could run like the beasts and lord it over all creation.

"With the help of his dog and horse, he tried to tame all wildness from the world. In his pride, he penned the blowing wind and streams to steal their strength. Then he fashioned an iron bit and reins to place in the wind's mouth so he could ride through the air like eagles.

"But the All rebelled against his wicked plan, rejecting tameness and loving the wildness at the heart of things.

"The earth spoke to her sister sky and they came together and gave birth to a daughter, Luna, which they placed in the heavens. There she grew round and fat and took her place among the stars, shedding light on those lacking sunlight and warm fire.

"Now the lion and fox and wolf could see their prey to hunt. The raccoons and possums could navigate the darkness, slipping under man's fences and taking his chickens and eggs to nourish themselves.

"To this night, we celebrate the moon's fullness by howling and prowling. And when she hides in darkness, leaving the night sky black and freckled with stars, we honor No Moon in silence and with humble gratitude.

"For on the day the Moon was born, she made a promise: that a time would come when wildness would rule the earth again, when natural strength would conquer the power of man's wit and animals would live again by might and cunning. Fences would fall and forests sweep over man's works, leaving wolf and lion to rule, as in days of old.

"When the moon grows horns," cried the coyote in a high-pitched quavering howl, "we celebrate the day when she will put on fur and fangs and come to us in the form of a giant Bear. On that day, flocks and herds will be dispersed and predator and prey dance again in sacramental union.

"Come now," the coyote called, eyes glistening. "Gather close as Little Rags brings the sacrifice."

Suddenly, the young raccoon appeared behind the coyote, clutching a hen by the neck. Gripping her throat firmly with both hands, he took her to the middle of the table, then held her toward the coyote, with averted face.

With a shock of recognition, Pip saw that the victim was Hetty, the senior hen. He watched with a mixture of horror and fascination as the young raccoon held the struggling hen toward the big coyote's mouth.

Quick as a wink, the coyote snapped his jaws and chopped the chicken's head off.

The crowd cried out in wild delirium as the raccoon lifted the headless body and held it over a clay bowl to drain its blood.

Pip watched spellbound as the red stream poured from the still-kicking carcass. Stars flashed inside his head, and a dull buzz filled his ears. He wondered if he were awake or merely dreaming. Ever since the coyote began speaking, Pip felt as if he were sleepwalking through a nightmare.

When the blood slowed to a trickle, the raccoon flung the lifeless body into the crowd. It arced above their heads and plunged into their midst, stirring the spot to turmoil. A cloud of feathers rose swirling above the communicants lunging for a taste of flesh.

While his congregation fought over the scraps, the coyote signaled his canine brothers to join him. When they'd all leapt up beside him onto the table, he dipped his face into the bowl and lapped up a portion of its contents. Then he raised his head and signaled the others to join him, eyes glowing like hot coals.

The foxes pressed their snouts into the bowl while Pip trembled on the edge of decision. He felt an overpowering urge to join, but held back till the scent of blood drew him forward, as in a trance.

Stepping up beside the foxes, he burrowed between them and lowered his head to drink.

When he raised his head a moment later, he nearly fainted with delight. The hunger that had been burning in his gut for weeks was suddenly gone. His body ached to flex its mighty sinews.

"To the hunt," rasped the coyote in his ear. "The chase is on!"

Pip turned to the voice and stared at empty space. The coyote had vanished like a shadow. The foxes had vanished, too.

Suddenly, Pip spied the white-tipped tail of Solomon disappearing around the corner. He heard claws clicking across the linoleum tiles of the kitchen floor as they raced toward the exit.

Pip bolted for the door just in time to see Solomon's tail vanishing through the swinging flap into darkness.

In a second, Pip was through the door himself, chasing after the foxes. Despite the shortness of their legs, they flew across the ground, softly panting. They appeared to be steering toward the nearby pond on the heels of the coyote, who loped across the grass with effortless speed.

Pip dug in his heels and ran faster, gaining on the foxes with every step.

Up ahead, steam rose from the pond, veiling the air with swirling wisps of vapor. Overhead, the moon shone down, revealing her yellow horns in the water's mirror. Pip could hear himself panting as he pulled beside the foxes, then heard their lungs pumping to the same rhythm as they ran in a pack, steering their silent course.

Up ahead, a file of large goslings scuttled over the grass toward the pond. The goslings didn't seem aware they were being chased. They were simply following what looked like an enormous humpbacked rodent.

Pip blinked his eyes. The goslings were trailing after Olivia, the possum who'd hijacked Gertrude's young. The thought flashed through his mind that he should let them waddle along safely to the pond. But that thought was driven out by a hunger deeper than the earth's molten core. No commandment etched on a wall could stop the longing that boiled up inside him. Hot blood and a horned moon spurred him to the chase.

Suddenly he realized that the coyote had made a tactical mistake by running up behind, to take the column from the rear. If not cut off, they'd spread their wings and flap the last yards to the pond, then run weightlessly across its surface.

In an instant, Pip saw what to do. He broke from the pack and angled toward the leader, who still hadn't sensed his approach. Hugging low to the ground, he raced to cut them off. He was ahead of the coyote, angling toward the possum from her left.

As he swooped in toward her, the possum startled and turned her face to his. But before she could flinch, he seized her neck in his jaws, swept her off the ground, and snapped her neck with a vicious double shake.

In panic, the goslings scattered, flapping their wings and skimming their feet along the ground. The foxes and coyote ran rings around them, chasing each by turn, till Pip swooped in, cut the stragglers off, and steered them toward the center of an imaginary circle. A nip here, a feint there, and the goslings were suddenly clumped together, bumping chests as they tried vainly to escape.

The coyote and foxes read Pip's intentions and closed around the trapped geese like a tightening noose. Within seconds, all seven lay dead and bleeding on the ground. Feathers were still settling amidst the carnage as the Canine Brotherhood moved in, to savor their victory.

For several minutes, the only sound was crunching jaws and cracking bones.

Looking up from his meal, the coyote grinned at Solomon.

"My friend, you said this young fellow had a gift. You are a very discerning fox."

The coyote turned to Pip.

"You have a talent, my friend. How do you think you would do at herding sheep?"

Pip puffed a feather from his lips and smiled.

"Sheep," he said, "are like these feathers. They go wherever the wind blows. And I'm a hurricane."

CHAPTER 37

By sunrise the next day, the extent of the carnage was still being tallied. Gertrude took command of the situation, rallying her friends and organizing search parties. First, she sent out the dogs to gather reports and measure the extent of the damage. Then she sent Pierre into the henhouse to calm the chickens and survey the destruction there. When the final tally was made, six hens, two chipmunks, and five half-grown chicks had been massacred along with the seven goslings and possum beside the pond. During the night, masked raiders with bushy tails had also stormed the henhouse, scattering its residents and stripping it of eggs.

Several others were still unaccounted for. Two possums in the orchard and a lamb had vanished without a trace. The dogs tried to track them down, but as usual, skunks had covered the marauders' retreat. The whole farm reeked of their colossal stink.

After a fit of anguish over her murdered young, Gertrude set her brains to work on how to save the farm. Last night's free-for-all was just a portent. If they didn't take action soon, the farm was lost.

Her first thought was to demand that the Council organize a raid on the farmhouse, where most of the forest-born lived, and expel them from the farm. But a discussion with the pigs convinced her of its futility.

"We're deadlocked—at best," said Bertha. "Three houses might vote in favor, but the other three are sure to vote against. Besides, everyone's too afraid to speak up now. Rumor has it anyone who does will get the same treatment as Raymond."

"Yep," snorted Barlow. "In these troubled times, no one will even vote. It's not just fear of getting called xenaphobic; they're afraid of retaliation.

"Just look at us," he sighed. "The missus and I have moved out of the pigpen. Ever since that ill-mannered boar moved in, no one's safe."

He paused to lick a fresh wound on his thigh.

"Yes," added Bertha. "When my husband confronted the lout about his bullying, he opened his leg with a thrust of that little tusk. And that traitorous son of ours applauded his behavior."

"Yes," sighed Barlow. "we'll be sleeping down at the barn with you tonight. That is, if you have room for two more rather portly bodies. We have been losing weight, though, thanks to our involuntary diet."

"I'm still worried about Pip," muttered Jessy. "It's almost time to work, and no one's seen him since yesterday."

"He'll turn up," Bertha said. "A strong young dog like that. He'll be all right."

"Things being the way they are, our only hope is to appeal to the law," said Shep. "We haven't had much luck with the new judge, but he's our only hope to put things right."

"Speaking of the judge," muttered Gertrude, "it's almost time to say goodbye to Emma. The judge said she had to leave by noon. At least the sun will be high, and all of the, er, new citizens asleep. Eudora took her to the front gate a while ago. The old ewe's in pretty bad shape. I thought she'd better have more company than those two foxes to send her off."

"Who can blame her?" asked Bertha. "Her exile's a death sentence."

"Her only chance is to make it to a farm," said Shep, tracing a paw through the dust. "I'll take her as far as I can, but I've got to get home by dark in case trouble starts."

When the group reached the dusty driveway, Shep made a shocking new discovery. The sign above the farm's front gate was down, leaving an empty stretch of autumn sky. Its shattered remnants lay strewn across the dust. The supporting post was chewed off and the sign had been scored and splintered by large teeth.

"Beavers," muttered Gertrude. "And to think we wanted them here to maintain the fences. Ha! If I saw one now, I'd stab out his beady eyes."

"Quiet," said Bertha, with a nervous glance toward the foxes. "Here's poor Emma and her guards."

The animals fell silent at the sight of their stricken friend. The poor old ewe looked utterly despondent. To avoid her guards, she'd already taken a few steps down the road toward exile.

Eudora, Gertrude, and Jessy cried openly, while Barlow hid his tears, for Emma's sake.

"It won't be so bad," he said. "With Shep, you'll be as safe as rain. You'll reach a farm, and some farmer will take you in. With all that wool, you'd make a fine addition to any flock."

"A few days' walk should get you to a town," Shep advised. "I once rode there in a car with Grover, to buy seed."

The poor ewe looked down the long road flanked by trees and stifled a sob.

"Those woods," she muttered, "that's what frightens me. They're dark and lonely and full of . . . pre-citizens."

A visible shudder rippled up her spine.

She turned to Shep. "Take care of the flock. Poor things, living in fear. I don't blame any of you, though. I just wonder, how did it get this way? Didn't we scare off that bear? Why do I have to leave my home for hurting some raccoon's feelings? We're brave. Why can't we do something?"

The old ewe sniffled. "But I'm not placing blame. You're all fine friends, fine friends. Especially you, Shep. No matter how you nipped and barked and chased, we always felt safe. I only wish I were back there now, with you dogging my heels. That was a safe kind of fear, not like what's down that road waiting for night to come. Oh, I better go now before I lose my courage. Good-bye, Gert. Barlow. Jessy. Eudora. Think of me when you can."

Now Shep had to fight back tears. He started to offer a last word of encouragement, but a harsh voice interrupted from behind.

"Better get going. It's past noon. Judge's orders."

Shep turned and glared at the hovering pair of foxes.

"I'll take her from here," he said. "Don't follow. If I see or smell anything suspicious—"

He looked them straight in the eye. "Go back to the barn," he growled. "Tell the judge his sentence has been carried out."

Shep followed Emma down the road, then turned back over his shoulder for a last word.

"And, foxes," he called, as they swiftly stole away, "when I get back tonight, you'd best stay clear of me."

CHAPTER 38

For days after the slaughter of innocents and Emma's forced exile, the farm animals huddled in a pocket of darkness behind the barn to vent their rage and frustration. Alone among the angry citizens, Pierre urged conciliation and restraint.

"Certainly, what happened the other night was terrible," said the duck, "but we must establish dialogue with the dissidents. They feel isolated, excluded. Their actions are merely a protest against injustice."

"What we need," muttered Barlow, "is to go in there and knock some heads. Why don't you go over there to Wilderness House right now, Pierre, and establish some law and order in that jungle?"

"Jungle?" sputtered the duck. "Sir, that is an outrage. That is just the sort of narrow-mindedness that has thrown our society into chaos. What we need is dialogue, sir, not demeaning epithets and threats of violence."

"Well, then," replied Barlow, "why don't you go over there and tell the foxes that you understand their protest and ask what we can do to help them assimilate to our farming way of life. It's almost dark. The place should be hopping soon. I'll walk over there with you, if you go in."

"That is an absurd proposal," scoffed the duck with a quick glance over his shoulder. "The farmhouse is a sensitive area. It's not safe even for the dogs to patrol. We have already marginalized its unfortunate citizens and abandoned them to disorder. How, then, can we expect them to conform to our notions of civil society?

"No, sir, it is useless to mock me with absurd proposals," said the duck. "My mates and I are emigrating. We are birds, after all. We can fly to friendlier climes. We will not stay here where injustice is perpetrated and resentment allowed to fester. We are leaving at dawn. Good-bye.

"I wish you well, my friends," the duck said, turning away. "We have enjoyed our life here, but the time has come to put our safety and happiness ahead of the needs of an unjust society. I regret that I can no longer offer you the wisdom of my counsel."

"Spoken like a true hero," sniffed Barlow as Pierre marched off toward the pond.

Then he called out after the swiftly departing duck, "I just hope we can face our next enemy without the terrible fury of your wrath."

The pig snorted with disgust and turned back to Eudora.

"I still wish the ducks would stay a bit longer," he said. "Our hearing with the judge is coming up. We'll need a sympathetic crowd—the bigger the better. Let's go inside and see how Gert and Shep are coming with our case."

Above the barnyard, the sky was growing dark. A full moon hung on the horizon like a silver plate as Bertha and Barlow strolled toward the barn with Eudora and Mara.

Suddenly, as they approached the door, a voice called from behind. "Wait, don't walk so fast. . . . Please take me with you. Before they see I'm gone."

Eudora turned and spied a tiny humped thing rushing toward them through the grass. It looked like a big rat, but as it drew closer, it proved to be a slender female possum.

"Take me inside," the possum pleaded. "Quickly. If they see, it'll be the end of me."

Eudora was puzzled by the possum's odd behavior, but felt stirred to help the poor helpless thing. The little possum was shaking all over and glancing back toward Wilderness House as if she expected a posse of wild coyotes to come charging out after her.

With the recent carnage still troubling her mind, Eudora felt her heart swell with pity for the harmless little creature.

"Come along," she said. "Just walk ahead of us. No one can see you there. We'll follow you to the barn."

That was all the encouragement the possum needed. She bolted toward the door and raced inside.

Once safely hidden behind a pile of straw, she thanked her new companions for their help.

"I can't tell you how grateful I am. You might not remember me, but I'm Ophelia. One of Oliver and Olive's young."

Then wringing her little hands, she cried, "Oh dear, oh, me, I'm done for, done for."

"What's the matter?" asked Mara, leaning down toward the pitiful little creature. "You seem to be in terrible distress."

"I've run away," the possum sobbed. "From Wilderness House."

She looked up at the giant mare and sniffled. "I don't want to be wild anymore. I want to be tame. It's terrible what's happening there. I couldn't stand it anymore."

"Couldn't stand what?" asked Eudora.

"The terror," the possum whispered. "The foxes and coyotes run everything. The rest of us have no say. If we want to stay alive, we follow orders and keep out of their way."

"You possums surely outnumber the foxes," said Eudora kindly. "Why don't you take your complaints to the Council. Every animal has a tongue and a voice, remember? Green Pastures Farm gives rights to all."

"To all," sniffed Ophelia. "To all the strong, you mean. Wilderness House has its own law. Cy says—he's the head coyote—that *tame* is just another word for *prey*. That's why I couldn't stay."

Suddenly stricken by fear again, Ophelia looked wildly about the barn.

"They say they'll kill anyone who betrays them. If they knew I was here, they'd swallow me down like a mouse."

The possum collapsed in a heap of sobs and shudders.

"There, there," said Eudora unsurely, "you're safe with us." She looked toward the wide barn door into the outer darkness, wondering how to allay the possum's fears.

Suddenly, the night's silence was shattered by a distant howl. It ululated through the night air like a bugle and echoed off the distant mountains.

The barn animals leapt to their feet into electrified consciousness.

"What was that?" asked Jessy, panting.

Still shaking off straw, Duke pricked his ears and said, "Sounded to me like a coyote."

"Not a coyote," said Shep, stepping forward. "Can't say for sure, since we're so far south, but you ask me, that's a wolf."

All eyes turned toward the widely gaping door.

"Maybe we should close it," whispered Barlow. "If what you say is true."

"Can't," said Shep. "We've got to go out there and bring in the sheep."

"Duke," he said, turning to the big Lab. "It's going to take all three of us. The cattle will have to fend for themselves."

"Jessy," he said, turning to his mate. "I'm sure Pip's safe with Bronson in the pigpen. We'll check later. Those sheep have got to come in."

"What if there's more than one wolf?" asked Eudora, eyeing her little friends.

"If there's more than one, that's trouble," Shep replied. "At least till we can rally the whole farm. Meanwhile, keep everyone inside and post some horses at the door. We've got to go. If the sheep scatter, there'll be a slaughter out there."

CHAPTER 39

The dogs rounded up the sheep and herded them to safety without encountering any further evidence of a wolf. Once the sheep were safely stowed in the barn, Shep went back to the pastures to alert the cattle and horses. He was surprised to see how calmly they took the news.

"A lone wolf would not dare enter this pasture," said Garth, barely raising his horns to eye the fence. "At least, not while I'm here."

Kit was almost as nonchalant as the bull.

"It would take a whole pack to bring down a creature my size," he said, surveying his rolling pastures. "A lone wolf can't stand up to these," he added, stabbing the dirt with a hoof. "If there's a wolf lurking about, I'll see he keeps his distance."

Back in the barn, the sheep huddled together, whispering among themselves till Shep returned. With a wolf running about, it would be days before it would be safe for the sheep to return to the pasture. The dogs could patrol the fences and sniff for trouble till it disappeared back into the wilderness. Till then, they'd have to make the best of things.

One benefit, though, of having the sheep forced into the barn, Eudora realized, was that for once the entire flock would attend the hearing.

"It's good we're all here together," said the old cow, moving among the barn's tightly packed guests. "It'll soon be time for Shep to convince the judge to kick those stinky skunks off the farm so we can have some law and order again. Strength in numbers, you know. Let every voice be heard."

As time passed, the animals grew increasingly bored with their confinement. Eudora was growing impatient herself. By the third night, the sheep were cavorting about the barnyard, asking when they could return to their pasture.

"I wish dear old Raymond were here," sighed Eudora, surveying the restive sheep. "He kept us all on time. I'm sure the judge was supposed to be here hours ago. Why doesn't he come?"

At last, the judge strode into the barn, surrounded by an entourage of fellow raccoons. He greeted his friends in the barn, then looked about for Shep and Gertrude, who were hastily summoned by Duke.

As soon as the pair arrived, the judge issued some preliminary instructions and mounted a hay bale to start the proceedings.

Horses and cattle were still pushing in through the door as Gertrude surveyed the crowd. Here in the tightly packed barn, the farm animals outnumbered the forest-born by a large margin. And the presence of the horses and cows provided a daunting spectacle to the little residents of Wilderness House still squeezing in through the door.

It soon became apparent that the barn was too small to hold everyone, so the judge ordered them all outside to the barnyard.

As Gertrude marched outside and saw the crowd there, her heart sank like an anvil.

Battalions of porcupines, muskrats, groundhogs, skunks, and weasels stood in massed ranks beside deer, raccoons, and possums. A train of new arrivals stretched from the barnyard all the way to the farmhouse door.

Peering over their heads to the outer rings of the crowd, Gertrude spied several foxes—and a pair of large coyotes—staring back at her with shining yellow eyes. Litters of young cubs frolicked about their feet as they leered at her across the teeming barnyard.

Shep nudged the goose with a quick poke of his muzzle.

"It's time," he whispered. "Get your mind back on the case."

As soon as the judge remounted his bale, Shep stepped forward and began his case.

"The problem I want to address tonight is skunks," he said, looking up at the judge. "As long as they're here stinking up the place, we dogs can't do our jobs. If we can't track down and identify criminals, we might as well not have laws here on the farm."

"Shep's right!" cried out a goose, and the farm animals bawled their assent. Shep turned from the judge and directly addressed the crowd.

"Everything we once loved about Green Pastures Farm is now threatened. Somebody's chopped down the sign at the farm's front gate. The one with the horse shoe," he added with a glance toward Kit. "Our winter stores are being stolen from under our noses. Our fellow citizens are being slaughtered in cold blood. Every day a hen or lamb is reported missing. And there's nothing we can do to find the perpetrators and bring them to justice.

"Your Honor," he said, turning back to the judge, "if we're going to maintain law and order, we have to take action—now. If you can send Emma into exile for uttering a wrong word, you can expel the skunks for obstructing justice and making a mockery of our laws."

A murmur of approval rippled across the barnyard, punctuated by howls and jeers.

"That's right," added Duke, stepping forward. "It's gotten so bad, my eyes hardly ever stop watering. We've got to kick out those stinky skunks before they ruin things for us all."

As the big lab retreated into the crowd, a skunk scurried forward and took the floor to reply.

"If this farm is being ruined," he shouted, glaring at Duke, "it's by xenaphobes like you. You big dumb mutt, what gives you the right to insult an entire species? We skunks have just as much right to be here as you."

The skunk's supporters cheered as several of his relatives scurried forward and lifted their tails at the crowd.

"How'd you like it if we sprayed the lot of you?" one shouted as the crowd shrank back. "How 'bout we hose you down and cool your tempers now?"

"No justice, no peace," cried a muskrat, vaulting forward. "No justice, no peace!" he repeated, cueing the crowd.

The barn animals cowered in terror as the skunks took aim and the crowd took up the muskrat's angry chant.

The judge called the court back to order by drumming on a large tin plate.

"Order!" he cried, "That's enough! That's enough! We will have order here."

When the crowd finally settled, he turned and addressed the little barn owl, who was presenting the opposition's case.

"Professor," he said with a nod, "keep it brief."

The little owl smiled up at the judge, then at the Wilderness faction, then at Gertrude, who'd taken refuge among the friendly dogs and pigs.

"I think our striped friends here have stated their case rather eloquently," said the Professor. "Let me begin, then, by simply reminding the court that Green Pastures Farm is a Many-Animalist society, and that in such a society laws are based not on the character or rights of individual citizens, but on the sovereign principle of biodiversity.

"In such a society," said the owl, "no exception can be made to the principle of inclusion. We should extend warm feelings to all of our fellow creatures—except, of course, the rogue species of crows, a vile, filthy bird, devoid of compensating virtues. As I said, we must tolerate the differences of others, and, instead of mocking their exotic shape or size—or smell—we should celebrate the singular virtues of each. . . ."

As the lofty phrases rolled off the barn owl's tongue, casting their spell over the mesmerized crowd, a hoarse voice interrupted.

"Excuse me, Professor. Just a minute, my learned friend."

The barn owl sputtered to a halt. "Er, ah, what, ah . . . Who the devil are you?" he demanded, glaring at the upstart fox. "I was speaking. Since when do vagabond canines of dubious origin presume to interrupt an owl of my, ah, rare distinction . . ."

Ignoring the owl's sputtered protest, Solomon stepped forward and softly addressed the judge.

"Your Honor," he said, looking up at the startled raccoon. "If I may, I would like to exercise my right as a pre-citizen and bring a formal charge against the owl. In calling the species of crows vile and filthy, he has committed an act of hate speech. On behalf of Wilderness House, I ask the court to place him under immediate house arrest."

"What?" sputtered the owl. "You are joking, of course. Accusing me—the champion of Biodiversity, the author of Many-Animalism—of, of HATE speech. As if it were possible for an owl of my unquestioned commitment to social justice to engage in such an act. . . ."

"The fox is right," interrupted the judge. "You did call them vile. And filthy, too."

"Well, yes, of course," sputtered the owl. "I was speaking—perhaps a bit too loosely—of some unfortunate tendencies of the breed . . . of their, uh, innate propensity to, well, to engage in certain antisocial acts and, perhaps to . . ."

"He just did it again," said Solomon. "He said crows were antisocial. That's xenaphobic."

The barn owl sputtered incoherent protests, then looked at the grinning fox and visibly sagged.

"I was, ah, referring merely to certain antisocial *behaviors*," he added hastily. "I hope I didn't imply—inadvertently—that my noble winged brothers are by, ah, their very nature . . . well, given to certain, shall we say . . ."

"Sergeant-at-Arms," said Rags, turning to the large raccoon beside him. "The law is the law. Please take the Professor into custody and lock him up in the barn."

The burly raccoon approached as the terrified Professor backed away.

As he edged toward the circling crowd, two possums leapt from their seats and seized the owl by the wings.

The prisoner didn't even struggle as they dragged him from the hearing to the barn.

"We'll deal with you later, Professor," called the judge over jeers and insults.

He turned back to the fox. "Mr. Solomon, the court thanks you for performing your duty. Now, if there are no other matters before the court—"

"Ah, there is one thing, Your Honor," said the fox with a courtly bow. "In addition to the matter of the skunks, there is the unresolved matter of the crows."

The fox turned to the crowd behind him.

"I would like to introduce my friend Kraven," he said, pointing to a large crow perched on a coyote's back. "Kraven is the leader of a local flock of crows—a very fine fellow, if I may say so. A bird of the utmost integrity."

As the fox introduced him, the crow bowed toward the judge, then turned and winked at his friends in the crowd behind.

Reluctantly, the judge settled back in his seat. "All right," he said, then signaled the fox to continue.

Solomon began his presentation by extolling the judge's wisdom and the farm's unfailing commitment to biodiversity. He brought the crowd to tears describing the shame and humiliation endured by skunks and crows at the hands of those who lacked a commitment to Many-Animalism. Then after a final tribute to biodiversity, he proposed that the skunks and crows be granted full citizenship on the farm.

When he finished, the crowd cheered wildly. The judge banged on his plate to quiet them. Then—without even pausing to deliberate—he ruled that the skunks and crows be allowed to stay.

Pandemonium broke out across the barnyard. In the confusion, Kraven stretched his wings, leapt from the coyote's back, and swooped three times above the judge's head to celebrate his ruling.

Gertrude was too stunned by the spectacle of her fellow citizens cheering this farce to voice even a feeble protest.

"We're already low on corn," muttered Barlow beside her. "By next summer, we'll be lucky to harvest a bushel with those crows about."

Utterly dejected now, the goose and pig turned toward the barn and wearily trooped toward their beds.

Suddenly, the fox leapt forward and called out to the judge, stopping them in their tracks.

"And now, Your Honor," he said over the clamor of shuffling feet, "I would like to call the court's attention to one last matter—an injustice that has troubled me since the night I first arrived, a lonely outcast, on this farm. I speak, sir, of the insidious practice of herding and flocking."

Gert turned around and stared in amazement at the fox's audacity.

"Such xenaphobic behavior on the part of the indigenous animals," declared Solomon, "is clearly unconstitutional. It has but one purpose: to exclude and marginalize. To stigmatize the forest-born as *Other*.

"The time has come," he declared with a swish of his white-tipped tail, "to end this unfair practice.

"And so, Your Honor, to ensure that all animals walk on the same level ground, flocking and herding must be abolished. All current flocks and herds must be broken up and distributed throughout the farm.

"In addition," the fox added, "to prevent further outbreaks, I propose that all citizens be educated in the dangers of *feralphobia*."

At the sound of the ominous word, a gasp rose from the crowd.

Then heads twisted toward neighboring heads and paws rubbed chins as the animals tried to guess what the strange word meant.

"What's feralphobia?" hissed Barlow in Gertrude's ear. "You're a teacher. What's feralphobia?"

For a moment the goose didn't answer.

"It means," she muttered through a tightly clenched bill, "fear of . . . wildness. It means that everything we believe in is about to become a crime. It means that if we don't do something soon, foxes and coyotes will be our lords and masters.

"It means," she said, staring glumly at the smugly smiling Solomon, "we're about to lose the farm."

CHAPTER 40

Gossip and news are the lifeblood of a herd or flock. Once driven from their comforting embrace, the animals of Green Pastures Farm could no longer effectively communicate, and so any hope of reestablishing the governance of the Animal Council was lost. In the absence of its authority, the farm's governance fell to the judge, who appointed a special committee of weasels and skunks to enforce the laws, which they did now with ruthless efficiency.

First, the committee placed foxes and coyotes in each of the farm's five houses to serve as "House Climate Monitors." The Monitors' job was to break up illegal gatherings and eliminate feralphobia in thought, word, and deed.

Outside the five houses, Kraven and his troop of crows patrolled the air to ensure that no herding took place. Whenever sheep or cows gathered in a yard or pasture, the crows swooped down and broke them up. If violators resisted, the crows called in Monitors to scatter them by force or haul them off to judgment in Wilderness House.

Within days of taking up residence on the farm, the crows took their revenge on the Professor. Attacking the owl by day when he was blind, they stabbed at his eyes and wing feathers till he fled out the hayloft window into daylight, zigzagging toward the shelter of the distant trees.

With the Professor gone, the judge appointed a new superintendent to run the school. To appease the forest-born, who demanded a role model for their young, he appointed Solomon, who had impressed the judge and his friends at the hearing with his fairness and wisdom. The fox immediately hired a staff of possums and beavers to instruct the swelling ranks of students who now trooped off to school each night into brave new realms of thought.

To break up the horses, Kit and Mara were moved from the stables to the barn, and deer transferred to the stables to join the last horses there. Only the cattle's herd remained intact. Garth refused to leave the pasture, and he and the cows were too big and ornery to scatter by force. Cy, the coyote who chaired the committee, threatened to cut off their winter grain if they didn't comply, but he quickly withdrew the threat when he realized that if the big bull wanted to, nothing could stop him from breaking into a silo or storage shed.

Still, the forest-born were often heard muttering about the bull's feralphobia and wishing for the day when Grandfather Bear arrived.

The hens and sheep had the hardest time adapting to life without flocks, wandering aimlessly about the farm till drawn like iron filings by magnetism back into larger groups. Whenever this happened, the foxes and coyotes reacted instantly, scattering them to the far corners of the farm with joyful whoops and howls.

The dogs did their best to comfort and protect their wandering friends. For his part, Pip said he'd distract the sheep from their loneliness by practicing his herding, and he was often seen chasing a bleating flock across the fields into the far corners of the farm. Despite the dogs' best efforts, though, the sheep seemed confused and despondent, and their number dwindled steadily day by day. Some said they wandered off into the forest. Others said they were being eaten by the Canine Brotherhood, whose members looked fatter and healthier every day.

The farm animals were so afraid of saying anything feralphobic that they no longer spoke their thoughts aloud. In the absence of open discussion, rumor flowed like a current through the farm, spreading fear and confusion with every whispered word.

According to a hen who had heard it from a horse who'd heard it in the pasture, members of the Canine Brotherhood cavorted nightly with their cousins in the woods. Some were even rumored to have mates and litters in the forest they visited by day as the farm slept.

A goose claimed that a chipmunk who lived in Wilderness House said the residents there now openly called themselves *wild*. Meanwhile, they called their farm-born neighbors "domestics"—or even "settlers"—contemptuously hurling the insults whenever they passed.

"I heard the judge is going to change the name of Green Pastures Farm to Wild Valley," whispered a sad-eyed cow. "The pre-citizens say that *pasture* and *farm* are feralphobic, implying separation from nature."

"Think that's something," snorted Barlow, "the big boar who drove us out of the pigpen used to call us trespassers. And that was on days when he was being nice."

"How can he say that?" asked an indignant hen. "I thought the word was banned."

"Banned for us," sniffed Barlow. "There's a different standard for them. Remember, we domestics have to be punished for the crime of being tame."

"It's not fair," insisted an old ewe named Ethel. "We're driven from our flocks while those foxes and coyotes run about in packs whenever they want. The next time I see them congregating, I'm going to tell them what I think."

The next evening, the old ewe proved good as her word.

Spying four red foxes conversing in the barnyard, she cried out loud enough for everyone to hear, "Break it up, boys. No herding or flocking. Hoof and paw on the same level ground, you know."

Two days later, her headless carcass was discovered behind the stables by Duke, who buried it on the spot.

"They took Ophelia back to Wilderness House," reported Eudora when the dogs returned. "Two big coyotes just marched in here and dragged her off, kicking and screaming, to Wilderness House. I hate to think what'll happen to her there."

"You think that's bad?" said a gosling. "Yesterday, they kicked all us females out of school. They say we're supposed to follow the lead of males, so we don't need an education."

"How can they do such a thing?" demanded Gertrude. "I started that school—and served as its first superintendent.

"If we don't do something soon," she muttered, "they'll soon be turning us out into the woods."

She glanced across the floor at the little red fox who served as the barn's Climate Monitor. Luckily, he was curled up in the corner, fast asleep.

"Fellow citizens," she whispered, drawing in her circle of friends, "I've had enough. It's time we put some iron in our spine. Starting tonight, I want each of you to spread the word. No more formalities. As of now, we're taking things into our own hooves and paws. Go out there and recruit every farm animal brave enough to make a stand. Tell them it's us against them. Our day is near.

"When those wild ones see us with fires in our bellies," she said with gleaming eye and loudly beating heart, "they'll run howling back to the woods where they belong."

CHAPTER 41

To spread the spark of revolt, Gert spoke to the birds and sheep. They suffered most under the new order. If she could stoke their discontent, she was sure it would spread across the farm like a prairie fire. And so, individually or in pairs, she met with her neighbors secretly—whenever she could elude the Monitors.

"If you want to live in flocks again, there's no use whining," she repeated with each visit. "We'll have to drive those wild ones out for good. If you love this farm, then stiffen your spines and move when you hear the signal."

"Should you be calling them *wild*?" whispered a ewe with a nervous glance toward the farmhouse. "Remember what happened to Emma."

"That's precisely what I'm talking about. Emma. What happened to her and what's happening to everyone," Gert replied stiffly. "Those wild ones have taken over the farm, and now they think they're our masters. Soon they'll make no pretense and just swallow us all down in a single feast."

"I don't know," muttered the ewe. "You saw what happened when Ethel stood up to those foxes."

"And I know what we did to that bear when he invaded the farm," Gert retorted. "Come on, girls, it's time to pull together and make a stand."

"Violence is never the answer," bleated a lamb.

"Yes, killing just perpetuates the violence," added her mother. "It's always right to die for a cause, but never to kill for it."

"Tell that to the foxes," Gertrude muttered as she stalked off toward the henhouse to try her luck there.

Shep was having no better results with Kit out in the pasture. Without the stallion's leadership, the mares wouldn't join, and without the horses, the fight for the farm was lost.

"Don't you see, Kit? They've taken down all the horseshoes and chewed up the sign. They're going to change the name of Green Pastures Farm forever. What's wrong with calling a pasture a pasture, or a farm a farm? It's ours, isn't it? We've worked and defended it. It's time to take it back."

Kit wrinkled his brow and chewed his hay thoughtfully.

"Solomon says that, by rights, the land belongs to all. That sounds pretty reasonable to me," the stallion replied. "We want to be inclusive, don't we? That's only fair."

"Oh, for goodness sake, stop listening to Cy and Solomon," Shep replied in exasperation, "and listen to your heart, for once."

"I'll give it some thought," replied Kit, dipping his head toward a hay bale. "Give me some time to think and I'll let you know in a while."

Shep and Gert joined forces to make their pitch to Garth. Though slow to act, once aroused, the big bull was a battering ram. If they planted the seed in his head, it would bloom in time. Once he saw the logic of their plan, he was bound to join the revolt.

"We've already got Kit and the horses," bluffed Shep. "You don't want them to steal the glory, do you? You're bigger than Kit, and your herd outnumbers his. You cattle can turn the tide and win the prize."

"Why should I get involved?" drawled Garth. "We're safe here in the pasture. We can trample those foxes and coyotes to dust anytime we want. You're an alarmist, that's what you are. I'll take my chances here in my own pasture."

Gert stepped up and looked the big bull in the eye.

"That's right, you're safe, so I guess that's all that matters. But safe for how long, you ever think of that? What happens if a mountain lion comes along someday? Or worse—a bear? One swat of his paw, and that thick skull of yours will crack like an eggshell. Ever see the size of a bear's claws? What would you do against *that*?"

"Aw, you're both exaggerating," replied the bull, turning his back to the wind. "If there's ever a real danger, I'll know what to do."

Back at the barn, the little band of revolutionaries gathered to review their progress and plan their next steps.

"Kit's thinking about joining," said Shep hopefully. "And Garth said he'll act when a real danger comes. That's a start."

He turned to Eudora. "How did it go with the pigs and milk cows?"

The old cow lowered her eyes and shook her head.

"Barlow and Bertha are with us. But the cows hurt from not being milked. They're in no mood for rebellion. They're still hoping to get the possums back. They don't want to stir things up till that point's settled.

"Besides," she sighed, "they're terrified of the coyotes. If I could just convince them we could return to the old ways . . . but all they can think of now is their swollen udders."

"Milk cows? What about me?" stammered Duke. "I'm starving to death. My stomach hurts so bad, I'm half tempted to join the Brotherhood. Yeah, that's right. The foxes are always telling me how much food they have over there. Someday I just might join them.

"Only thing is," he added glumly, "I want to stick with my friends."

Silence settled on the circle like a chilling fog.

"What we need," said Eudora finally, "is something to fire up their memories. They're all so beaten down. If we could just show them the path, I'm sure they'd follow. At least, the older ones would. I'm not so sure about the young."

"That's it!" cried Gert. "It's almost time for the pageant. If we could reenact our victory over the bear . . ."

"Aw, we tried that already last year," replied Duke. "You saw the mess they made of that."

"Besides," said Eudora, "you couldn't put on the play. They won't let you anywhere near that school."

"This time it's different," insisted Gert, now starting to pace. "I just talked to Pip. He's running the show this year. I'll convince him to put on my play. I remember it word for word, like it was yesterday. He's the brightest one in the lot. He could learn the thing by heart in no time at all. And when it comes time to perform it, he can get sympathetic friends to play the main parts."

The other animals remained skeptical, but once a thing got into Gert's head, there was no getting it out. She was convinced her play would rouse the farm to action.

"We'll spread the word," she said excitedly. "When the play ends, that'll be the signal. We'll all shout 'No Trespassing,' like before. When the crowd picks up the chant, that's when we move. We'll start the attack against the Monitors.

"Once we beat them" she said with a firmly set bill, "the rest of that crew will have to turn and run."

CHAPTER 42

On the night of the pageant, Gertrude tingled from head to foot. Pip had memorized her play in record time and could now recite it from first to last like a seasoned actor. For the last week, he and his fellow students had been practicing their lines in the pigpen, which had been given over to the troupe for their rehearsals.

Tonight, though the air was cold and misty, the barnyard was packed with excited spectators. All the animals except Garth and his herd were gathered there.

As Gertrude wriggled through the crowd toward the front, she listened in on passing conversations.

"Horned moon," said a raccoon, nudging his friend. "Are you excited?"

"I'm getting goose flesh," the fox replied, provoking giggles.

"Look," cried a little lamb, "that dog is leading the actors into the yard. It must be time to start."

As Pip and the other actors took the stage, he spotted Gert and gave her a little wink.

Gert's heart leapt at the thought of what lay ahead. Her play could stir the dullest heart to action. With her friends placed strategically throughout the crowd, they were well positioned to act when the moment came.

Kit and the mares stood a few horse-lengths from the stage. From there, they could turn and charge the Monitors—or scatter them to the four corners of the farm. The dense crowding effectively nullified the ban on herding. The sheep and milk cows were packed in tight platoons, well positioned to move at her signal. The dogs, from their position at the rear, could survey the field of action, cut off escape, or flank the enemy in sudden counterattacks.

Gert was so caught up in her dream of victory she missed the opening lines of her own play.

She was startled back to attention by the sight of a young raccoon standing over a seemingly dead possum, who was covered from head to toe with clay dust to make him look like a man.

" . . . and when the naked ape lay dead on the farmhouse floor, the animals stood quivering in terror. So long had they worn their master's yoke, they no longer remembered who or what they were. Instead of leaping with joy at their deliverance, they cowered in the barn, howling laments."

"They might have joined their brothers in the forest," said a chipmunk, stepping forward into the moonlight. "They might have torn down the walls that penned them in. They might have opened their hearts and silos to their starving brothers in the forest. But these cold and miserly creatures hardened their hearts and hoarded their wealth like their cruel master, man."

From behind his back the chipmunk produced an acorn, which he held above his head to represent food.

"While little fawns and cubs starved through the winter," said a doe, stepping delicately forward, "the farm animals guarded their hoard like hungry dogs. They filled their bellies with corn and eggs and apples, congratulating themselves on their foresight and bravery."

"Growing louder and more militant each day, they marched in goose-stepping herds and giant flocks," cried a young beaver, pounding a fist against his palm. "They practiced the arts of war on a massive scale. Then, to better serve their greed, they enticed the humble creatures of the forest into their walled fortress with promises of wealth and security."

"But instead of treating their brothers as friends and equals," added a skunk with a flourish of his striped tail, "they forced the innocents to labor in their orchards. They drove them into the fields to harvest grain. They treated them with hatred and contempt, denying them even the warm comfort of their houses."

"But it was not enough to burden their bodies under heavy yokes," cried a fox, staggering beneath a phantom load. "These cunning animals aped their master's ways, putting reins on thought and leashes on natural instincts.

"*Tameness*, they called this pampered servility. *Domesticity*, they called this lack of animal vigor. They proposed to spread this religion of the weak throughout the world, to bring all of nature under its dominion."

"In this unnatural scheme," declared a sturdy eight-point buck, "the cows used clever signs scratched on wooden walls to master bulls. Geese dictated terms to passive, witless ganders. Raised up by herd opinion to high office, the puniest hen lorded it over the dog and duck, and the sow ate before the pig at the high feast. To walk on level ground, they would lay low mountains and have the mighty lion prostrate himself before the lowly lamb."

"But nature will not be mastered by herd opinion," declared a tall coyote pup. "She has rebuked those spiteful lies they called commandments. Claw and tooth will never submit to web and hoof. Nor strength walk on level ground with the bleating flock."

"The fences that locked out nature have fallen down," declared Pip, stepping forward with a sudden howl. "The heavy yokes have fallen from our backs, and the iron bit been rejected from our mouths.

"Called to the hunt by the horned moon this dark night, we stand ready to own the daylight as the darkness. This very night will see prophecy fulfilled. Grandfather Bear will come to smash your profane temples and spill the unlawful bounty from your bins. Nature herself will rush into the vacuum and power at last be restored to the long-exiled.

"Listen, my friends, and you will hear the dispossessed crying from the dark depths of the forest. Listen to their anthem as they march in triumph into battle, and join them in their chorus as they cry,

"*Take back the land! Take back the land! Take back the land!*'"

Dumbstruck by this sudden turn of events, Gertrude stared in astonishment at the crowd. It wasn't just the wild ones bellowing. Possessed by a mindless ecstasy, the young farm animals shouted along beside them. Grown ewes and cows and geese chanted along with a chorus of skunks and possums.

Suddenly, a piercing cry cut through the still night air—a long, snarling, protracted feline howl that stunned the crowd to silence.

In its silent aftermath, hooves shuffled and stamped in desperation. Horses whinnied and reared back, kicking the air.

Nostrils flaring, Kit tossed his head, looking wildly about with white-rimmed, bulging eyes.

A second yowl sent the rabbits and deer leaping toward cover. Groundhogs and chipmunks scampered for their lives. Sheep scattered in all directions, driving hens and possums before their thundering feet.

Beyond the barnyard, Gert saw dark shadows gliding across the fields on silent haunches. At the sight of them, the horses bolted toward the farmhouse and the gravel road beyond.

Gert looked over the heads of her swiftly fleeing allies for the trio of dogs and spied their tails bouncing toward the old fence line as they raced to confront the shadows galloping toward them from the woods.

Across the barnyard, foxes and coyotes pursued the fleeing pigs and sheep, pausing in their chase here and there to seize and snap the neck of a goose or hen.

"Hey, Gert, how'd you like the play?" rasped a voice close to her ear.

Gert turned and saw Pip leering hungrily, flanked by Little Rags and the fox called Solomon.

"School's out, old girl," said Solomon with a toothy smile. "No use resisting."

"Looks like your goose is cooked," snickered Little Rags, reaching out a paw.

As animals fled the mayhem in the barnyard to the fields, panic spread to the distant pasture, where Garth and his small herd of Hereford cattle were huddled against the dark. Despite the big bull's admonitions to hold steady, the cattle scattered at the sight of impending danger, running wildly about the field in all directions.

Alone now, Garth stood silent and unmoving as a stone. His curved horns gleamed in the moonlight as he faced the edge of the field, where a tall dark shape shambled toward him out of the forest.

"Grandfather Bear," whispered a coyote in the hush.

In the distance, Garth heard the ferocious roar of canine combat—growls, snarls, yips, and painful howls; the snap of jaws, the thunder of slamming chests.

Stiffening his legs beneath him like four pillars, Garth quivered from head to tail as the bear approached.

Far overhead, above the bloody mayhem, the horned moon shone in the sky like a crooked grin. A little barn owl caught its gleam on his feathers as he circled the barnyard, eyeing the scene below.

Ignoring the general carnage, his eye was drawn to a lone chick skittering across the barnyard toward a shed.

With a soft chuckle, the owl circled lower, thrust back his wings, and fell like a thunderbolt.

Printed in the United States
by Baker & Taylor Publisher Services